The National Short Story Prize 2006

The National Short Story Prize 2006

ATLANTIC BOOKS
LONDON

First published in Great Britain in 2006 by Atlantic Books,
an imprint of Grove Atlantic Ltd.

1 2 3 4 5 6 7 8 9

A CIP catalogue record for this book is
available from the British Library.

ISBN 1 84354 521 7

Printed in Great Britain by [tbc]

Atlantic Books
An imprint of Grove Atlantic Ltd
Ormond House
26–27 Boswell Street
London WC1N 3JZ

Contents

Preface

In the last twenty years or so the short story in Britain has come to seem like an artefact of a different era, or a memory of childhood. A snapshot of the late 1970s might show children growing up with *Jackanory*; Roald Dahl's *Tales of the Unexpected* sitting on the average household bookshelf; fiction readers leafing through the stories of V.S. Pritchett, Angela Carter or Ian McEwan. There was a market for stories, in the form of general interest magazines, women's glossies, or literary periodicals; they were standard material for television and radio adaptations; they were assumed to be a natural function, as it were, of the fictional urge.

A glance at the longer history of short stories would show, of course, that there was nothing especially natural about them. They were a modern confection, born of economic circumstances. Short stories had come to mass market prominence in the nineteenth century as a product of a boom in magazine publishing and, for much of the twentieth century, were assumed to be a perennial feature of the landscape. But if the conditions ceased to be favourable, there was no reason why stories should continue to be favoured. Towards the end of the 1980s, women's magazine's stopped publishing them, literary journals ceased to exert an influence and, by the 1990s, it was common to hear publishers say that story collections just didn't sell.

While the fortunes of the short story fell, those of the novel soared. The increasing importance of fiction prizes, principally the Booker and Whitbread, confirmed that if a writer sought recognition in Britain, the novel was the form with which to acquire it. This has not been the case in America, where the short story remains a bulwark of literary industry, capable of creating new reputations and sustaining old ones. But, for no very good reason, British admiration of the long American novel has not also extended to the short American story.

Is it possible, now, to begin talking about a revival? At a basic level, this year's inaugural National Short Story Prize is an attempt to fill a gap in the British awards market. The idea for it was conceived after the Arts Council launched a salvaging mission in 2002, called the 'Save Our Short Story Campaign'. As a result of this, *Prospect* magazine seized the opportunity to begin publishing short stories on a regular basis, joining a small group of mainstream publications that includes *Granta*, and very few magazines besides. The response from writers, readers and publishers was widely enthusiastic, sometimes grateful, occasionally almost plaintive. Why weren't more magazines publishing stories? Why was so little attention given to them? It was clear that something else was needed. So *Prospect* devised an award that would be big enough to stand alongside the Booker and Whitbread and generate that kind of attention for the short story. The next step was to find the right collaborators.

There is one place in Britain where the story does still find a major audience. BBC Radio 4 is the largest commissioner and transmitter of short fiction in the world. With the BBC broadcasting the shortlist of five stories contained in this anthology, and with £15,000 going to the winner, the National Short Story Prize now stands as the biggest award in the world for individual stories. (£3,000 goes to the runner up, and £500 each to the others on the shortlist.) The partnership behind the prize covers all the principal areas of production: a leading generalist magazine (*Prospect*), a national broadcaster (Radio 4), a publisher for the anthology (Atlantic Books), and a sponsor dedicated to supporting cultural and economic innovation – The National Endowment for Science, Technology, and the

Arts (NESTA). Meanwhile, the prize is administered by the Booktrust in England and the Scottish Book Trust, which jointly manage the ongoing 'Story' campaign, providing information and support to writers and readers nationwide (www.theshortstory.org.uk).

These are the mechanics of the prize; but they don't properly describe its purpose. At a deeper level, it is an attempt to have an argument about what a short story is – starting with what it is not. And what it is definitely not is a poor cousin of the novel. Stories are no more short novels than novels are long stories. Edgar Allan Poe, for one, considered the novel to be the inferior of the two forms, because its diffuse nature makes it incapable of conjuring a complete world. 'The ordinary novel is objectionable,' he wrote, 'since it cannot be read at one sitting, it deprives itself of the immense force derivable from totality.'

So what exactly is a short story? And can the short story as a literary form really be dying out in Britain? The first question is buried in the origins of human grammar and will keep being answered for as long as language survives. The second question is more simply addressed. The evidence of the first year of the National Short Story Prize has been that, where the short story has a place to go, it thrives. The five shortlisted stories contained in the following pages are written by authors who are invested in the form entirely and who generate worlds to be inhabited totally.

William Trevor is an undisputed elder statesman of the form; here, in 'Men of Ireland', he seizes the contemporary reality of a country in transition, glimpsed through the jaded eyes of a homeless man who can never properly leave home. Rose Tremain's stories exist in a wholly different region of the imagination to the historical panoramas of her novels; it is the eerie, closed world of an England just vanished that is chiselled into near-perfect shape in 'The Ebony Hand'. Meanwhile, if anyone is at the vanguard of the current Scottish story, it is Dutch-born Michel Faber; his tale, 'The Safehouse', belongs not so much to another world, as to an alternative universe. James Lasdun habitually writes about America with a cool English eye, and England from a withering American perspective; in 'An Anxious Man', the social and financial niceties of Lasdun's American world teeter on the brink of existential terror. Born in England and now living in Dehli, Rana Dasgupta is the relative newcomer in this anthology; he describes his first novel, *Tokyo Cancelled*, as a 'story cycle', and his vision of Lagos here, in 'The Flyover', is a distillation of fantasy and tragedy only feasible in the world of the short story.

These five were selected from over 1,400 entries submitted by writers who are British residents or citizens, all of whom had a prior record of publication. It would be premature to suggest from this that the short story has already entered a period of revival. But the signs are there, and this may be a beginning. Crucially, a renewal of interest needs to develop into new avenues of publication. Like any art, the short story needs to flourish among varied audiences and be disciplined by critical scrutiny. The short story is the purest modern expression of the most elemental of cultural activities. It seems strange that, in this storytelling island of all places, it should have become so rare.

Alexander Linklater
Deputy & Fiction Editor, *Prospect*

For full results of the 2006 National Short Story Prize see www.prospect-magazine.co.uk,
or www.theshortstory.org.uk

The Flyover
Rana Dasgupta

In the city of Lagos there was once a young man named Marlboro. He lived in a small room on Lagos Island near to the hustle and bustle of Balogun Market with his mother and two elder brothers.

The eldest brother was devoted to learning, and managed to get money together to go to a reputable university in India. The second brother had a friend who ran errands for rich people; they set up a booth together on Victoria Island: 'Bills paid. Visas made. No more stress. Trustworthy service: receipt always given. No job too big or too small!' Soon the commute became too much and he set up a bed in his stall. Marlboro was alone with his mother.

'Why don't you go and improve yourself like your brothers?' she would say. She worked long hours in a beer parlour and had no time for Marlboro's laziness.

He would lie on her bed while she was out, under a crinkled poster of Jesus standing on a rainbow saying 'Blessed are the poor in spirit: for theirs is the kingdom of heaven', and he would watch the lizards sitting on the fluorescent tube waiting for flies. 'If you can only find your own fluorescent light to sit on,' thought Marlboro, 'then everything comes to you.'

In fact everything did come to Marlboro; for he was generally thought to have Authority, and his evenings were full with people bringing him cups of ginger juice or measures of whisky in return for advice on how they could improve their luck in business or love. Everyone talked to him, discussed who was making money and how, who was honest and who was a cheat, and one person's problem always turned out to be the next person's solution. He gained a Reputation.

'Why don't you tell me who my father was?' Marlboro would ask late at night as his mother put up her cerise-toenailed feet that perfectly matched her cerise lipstick and flicked between soap operas, turned up to full volume to cover the scream of the flyover outside.

'Maybe if you make something of your life I will. It can't do anyone any good right now.'

'Maybe if I knew who my father was I would make something of my life.'

There was certainly an unaccounted-for influence in his mother's fortunes: for how could a woman with her income and status start spending her mornings at the Air Hostess Academy learning how to fly in planes? Surely it could not be her undeniable beauty alone that allowed her to cheat fate so dramatically; how could she suddenly be taking flights to Riyadh, Johannesburg, New York, and London? Marlboro affected indifference towards the vile speculation about his mother's ruses that arrived on his doorstep every evening, but was secretly mystified at how it had all happened. She would return with bars of Swiss chocolate that she would eat delicately in front of the National Geographic channel, giving only listless hints of endless avenues of glinting shops in return for Marlboro's circuitous questioning.

One evening while she was away in Frankfurt or Rome a one-eyed man came to the door and handed Marlboro a business card. 'Come. Tomorrow. Mr Bundu would like to make a proposition.'

Mr Bundu offered Marlboro whisky, which he gladly accepted, and sat him on a greasy red velvet sofa. 'I have heard about you. Seems you have Authority. A Reputation. Wondering how I can make use of that.'

'What business are you in, Mr Bundu?'

'Think of the flyovers by Balogun Market. Near your house. What a bazaar under those cement awnings! Do you know how much cash changes hands? Monument to the human spirit, Marlboro, the buzzing conversation of trade. But if you laid out all the great chains of being that end up in a place like that – you know what I'm saying. Moon and back several times. Complexities will strain your mind. Who owns which traders, who's got the monopoly on buses or prostitutes, which foreign company is the government trying to impress with seizures of locally-made versions of their products, who's Hausa, who's Yoruba, who owns the police chief, which products are producing inadequate returns on all this space, whose supply just dried up in Taiwan, who's behind the latest Surulere movie, who has bought the blindness of the most eyes… Phew! It's a whole universe. It *is* the whole universe. A worthy challenge for the intellect, don't you think?'

'You're very right, Mr Bundu.'

'It's a scintillating world; it's a pyramid of mercury: and we have to be standing on the top. Don't want to be paying out too many cuts to people above us. We want to collect them all ourselves. I work for a very powerful man, Marlboro. That's him in the picture.'

On the wall was a photograph of the multi-millionaire businessman Kinglord Bombata shaking hands with the French Prime Minister. Kinglord was wearing king-size Gucci sunglasses, and Marlboro thought to himself, 'There is a man I could look up to.'

'Mr Bombata is like you and me, Marlboro. Likes good systems. Doesn't like it when there are leaks. "Get me ten per cent of all the deals in those markets, Bundu," he says. But we need more information, Marlboro. Strategic thinking. I have boys who are very committed, they've done some great work, but the money's just not coming in. You have a Reputation, Marlboro. Do you think you can help?'

'I certainly do, Mr Bundu. It would be an honour.'

When Marlboro's mother next came back home he announced to her that he finally had a job, working for Mr Bundu.

'You'll get yourself killed, Marlboro.'

'No I won't. My survival instinct is impeccable.'

'You don't know what you're playing with. I don't know why I keep coming back here for you.'

The next time, she did not. Marlboro never saw her again.

Marlboro threw himself into his work and quickly proved to be a valuable asset to Mr Bundu's enterprise. In the evening sessions with his friends he probed deeper into their businesses and acquaintances and political intelligence, and became more impatient with those who were not useful. He took a number of people in the locality into his confidence and asked them to report to him on the things they heard and saw – the old-time owner of the manioc stall just outside his house, the night watchman, a policeman he had known since childhood... Each night he would have confidential phone conversations with Mr Bundu in which he passed on an astonishing array of information about upcoming police raids and political alliances. On the strength of this, Mr Bundu began to play a bold but methodical game of elimination. Systematic bus burnings frightened the public away from the transport system run by one competitor. Another organization that was planning its own rout of Mr Bundu's network was struck one night with a series of brutal attacks on key personnel, leaving it depleted and incredulous. Mr Bundu started to pay Marlboro a modest wage that allowed him to keep his mother's room.

With one woman gone from his life, two more quickly entered it.

The first existed only in his mind. Asabi, he called her, and she began to waft into the moments between sleep and wake, dropping a slow-falling gossamer veil over the world that shut out the whine of the okadas and all the barking merchants fighting for space under the flyovers, and left just sweet conversation. She appeared dressed in long Yves Saint-Laurent evening dresses with blue coral beads at her neck and a gele wrapped into a fantasy around her head, and she sat in marble houses with trees and verandahs. 'Marlboro,' she would say, 'you are doing well for yourself. Soon you will be out of your troubles, you will have space in this city to call your own, space for your mind to expand in; you will have houses and cars, and women will desire you. Your mother left too soon: if only she had been here to see this! And your father would be proud too: of that I am sure.'

'But who is my father?'

'Oh, Marlboro, why do you ask such questions? Fear not: for I am here, and in you I am well pleased. I will take care of you.'

And there was another new arrival in his life; for one day, as he was standing at a distance and watching the police seize all the stock of a CD and DVD trader who had fallen foul of Mr Bundu's machinations, a young girl marched straight up to him and stood impudently in front of him, considering his face.

'I can see two of me in your sunglasses!'

Marlboro did not quite know what to say.

'Who are you?' he ventured.

'Ona.'

'How old are you?'

'Fourteen.'

'You look much younger.'

'Well, I'm not.'

'Where are you from?'

'Southeast. Just come to town. I'm going to be a movie star.'

Ona came to live with Marlboro and he became very happy to have her around. He would wake her in the morning with a steaming plate of fried banana, fresh from the market, and when his work was finished they would talk long into the night until Ona fell asleep curled up under his arm.

'I'll take care of you, Marlboro,' she would say. 'You won't be in this room forever. With the traffic roaring by your ear. I'll take you out of here.'

'You'll forget me,' he said, with mock self-pity.

'I won't forget you, Marlboro. Maybe I'll even marry you.'

'You're like my little sister, Ona. I can't marry you.'

'Let's come back to this conversation in a couple of years' time when I'm the hottest property in Surulere and you can't move under those flyovers of yours without seeing life-size pictures of me. In my latest role: the beautiful and tragic African queen abducted into slavery by a cruel but handsome white man. You'll wish then you'd never said you couldn't marry me. All the folks in Victoria Island will be trying to get me to their garden parties just so they can see what I look like in real life. You'd better behave, Marlboro, and maybe I'll let you come with me.'

Whenever Marlboro made a little money he would put one hundred naira in an envelope and send it to her with a note:

dear ona. everyone is talking about you in
hollywood. when are you going to make your first
movie? i can't wait to see it. i hope the enclosed
will help you on your way. in love and admiration,
steven spielberg. ps don't tell anyone but i only
watch nigerian movies.

or

dear ona. it is with considerable excitement that we
apprehend from our courtiers that you are to be
a great star. unfortunately things are not what they
used to be here in england and this is all we
are able to spare for now. we hope it will be of
assistance. please come to buckingham palace
when you are next in the area. yours sincerely,
hm the queen of england.

'You are such a darling,' said Ona to Marlboro on
reading the Queen's dedication.

'I don't know what you're talking about,' he replied.

One morning, when Marlboro walked out to buy breakfast, he saw an army of policemen clearing the traders
from under the flyover with sticks: there was no time to
grab all the merchandise and they were wrapping what
they could carry in sheets, but the ground was littered
with spilled fruit and smashed VCDs as the police

shouted down complaints and arguments and city workers shovelled the debris of scattered digital watches into
the back of a truck. Marlboro watched in dismay.

'What is happening?' he asked the manioc seller.

'Government's made a decision. This market is caus-
ing too much violence in the city. It has to go. Local
businesses are complaining. They're clearing everything out; they'll brick up the whole space. The flyover
won't have any ground under it anymore; it will be an
empty fortress with holes for cars. You'll have to move
on, Marlboro.'

He telephoned Mr Bundu in a panic.

'I know, I know. For my man with his ear to the
ground you're a bit late. Come to my office straight
away.'

Marlboro ran to the Balogun Market office and sat
down, breathless and sweating, on Mr Bundu's velvet
sofa.

'I think we may have lost it, Marlboro. I had a private
telephone conversation with Mr Kinglord Bombata
early this morning. He is of the opinion that the flyovers are lost. Once the government makes a move like
this, it will never back down. Lose face. They'll brick up
that space and there'll just be big ugly walls there
with acres of land inside that no one can use. What a
tragedy, Marlboro: what a fine place that was.'

Marlboro nodded uncertainly.

'At the same time,' Mr Bundu continued, his face extravagantly grim, 'Mr Bombata views this incident as a personal attack by the government on his interests, and such attacks must be met with the ferocity they deserve. I am sure you have an idea of the kind of money that we have lost over this. Such things cannot be allowed to happen again. Wouldn't you agree?'

'I most certainly would, Mr Bundu.'

'Thank you for your support, Marlboro.' Mr Bundu laid a hand on his shoulder. 'You are a pillar of the organization. A source of great personal strength, I might add.'

He went to a drawer, took out a handgun and placed it on the table.

'We all know which Commissioner is responsible for this, and we know very well what despicable motives he has for opposing Mr Bombata's ambitions. For him to continue unpunished would not be good public relations for our organization. I have decided that you will kill him. There's no one else I can trust with such a mission, Marlboro. You will do it tonight.'

Marlboro looked at him in horror.

'But such a mission is certain death! No one who tries to break into a Commissioner's house with a gun will come out of it alive.'

'I will take care of the guards, Marlboro. You will not face any opposition. Don't worry.'

'With all due respect, Mr Bundu, and I know you have been very good to me, but is it not relevant that I am not a marksman, have rarely handled firearms? I am not certain I am even capable of this.'

'Let me remind you that all of us are in this fix because of your failure to do your job. And since you force this conversation into such a corner, since you demand of me these totally uncalled-for explanations, I should let you understand, let me be blunt, that death at the hands of the Commissioner's guards is as nothing compared to the perils that would await you should you refuse to comply. Kinglord Bombata's fury is not a little thing. I am offering you an opportunity to vindicate yourself in his eyes.'

Marlboro continued to stare, trying to take in his situation.

'I think that is all we have to say to each other, Marlboro. Be gone.'

Sick with fear, Marlboro drew all the curtains, took to his bed, and lay under a blanket in the solace of darkness. While Ona brought him water and sang pop songs to soothe him, Marlboro drifted in and out of a feverish sleep. Asabi came to him in a breath of silk and he reached out to her in relief.

'Asabi I am so afraid! I cannot do this thing.'

'Marlboro you must do your duty. Be strong!'

'I will do as you say, and not as I feel, for my mind is lost and I can no longer reason. But please tell me if I am going to die. Am I going to lose you and Ona and the precious life we have?'

'Have no fear, Marlboro. We will see each other again soon.'

He woke up and it was dark. Ona lay asleep by his side. He shook her.

'Let me sleep!' she moaned.

'You can sleep later. I have to go out now. I want to give you a kiss.'

He kissed her on the forehead and looked at her face for a long time.

'You will be a great star, Ona. I am sure of that.'

He went to the door and opened it, and turned to look back at her one last time.

'Always remember…'

But he couldn't think how to finish the sentence. He walked out into the street.

Outside he saw that the wall around the former market under the flyover had already been built up to a height of nearly three metres. He could not believe how fast they had worked. In another day or so it would rise to meet the arch of the road passing overhead and everyone would forget that there had once been a bustling marketplace behind those forbidding stones.

He took an okada to a spot near the Commissioner's house and walked the rest. He walked stealthily in the shadows, tried to spy a way in through the walls of the massive mansion, smoked a cigarette as if he were just taking a break... A man appeared from nowhere and took his arm gently; it was one of the Commissioner's guards. Marlboro made ready to struggle.

'Don't worry, sir. Mr Bundu has seen to everything. We are at your service. This way.'

He led Marlboro through the spiky steel gates and up the drive, stiff men with AK-47s nodding confidentially as they passed. He opened the front door and let Marlboro in.

'Good luck.' He gave an encouraging smile.

'Thank you,' Marlboro replied, though no noise came from his mouth.

He tiptoed through the marble vestibule, the house opening out above him into bedrooms and reception rooms and verandahs; he looked in through a doorway and there was the Commissioner sitting at a desk, reading the newspaper. He drew his gun and pointed it, holding it outstretched with two shaking hands while the Commissioner sat in the comfort of his own home and idly turned another page, while he frowned down at the news through his bifocals; how could he shoot a man reading the newspaper? And he coughed so the Commissioner looked up and of course he was surprised but he acted calmly, took off his glasses, and put them on the desk, smiled somewhat tensely at Marlboro, stood up halfway and gestured towards the sofa, 'Why don't you have a seat?' and Marlboro pulled the trigger.

The noise was like a natural disaster breaking into the quiet, but the bullet made a calm, neat hole in the Commissioner's forehead and he fell cleanly into an empty space on the floor. Marlboro looked dumbly at him: he was smaller than he looked in life and below the desk his shirt had been untucked. The gunshot still seemed to be echoing somewhere in the house, for silence had not returned and there was a rushing in Marlboro's head; and as he watched, as he tried to right himself, there flowed out from behind the dead man's ear, there flowed out onto the marble a single thin stalk of blood that lost its surface tension at the end and spread out into a flower, a perfect orchid in blood arching around the dead man's head; but there was no time to lose and was there not in fact someone calling through the tornado, saying again and again, 'Marlboro!' and he followed the voice up the stairs and into a bedroom where a woman lay decorously on the bed, flicking through snapshots; and it was Asabi.

'Asabi! What are you doing here?'

'Come and lie with me, Marlboro. You have done well tonight.'

'I don't understand you anymore, Asabi. I don't understand what you want me to be.'

'Come and lie here. You must be exhausted.'

And he lay down and wished for comfort and Asabi smelt fragrant and he looked at the photographs she was holding. 'I just found these lying around, Marlboro,' she said. They were old photos, there was the Senator standing proud in younger days, there were people all around dancing in the house of marble and trees and verandahs, and his arm was round a woman, a woman who used to wear cerise lipstick even in those days, and it was his mother, and there she was again lying naked on a bed, on that same bed where he now lay! And Marlboro looked at Asabi and said, 'No', and she looked long at him and said 'I don't think you should jump to any conclusions. Your mother was a fine-looking woman. Probably had other men than this one.'

She kissed him reassuringly; and then suddenly looked serious.

'You should be going, Marlboro. You need to stay in control. This is not a good place for you to be. You should leave.'

She ushered him away and he began to remember his situation. He walked out onto a verandah and could see the police assembling in the street, preparing to surround the house; he leapt from the verandah into the

garden of the house next door, and somehow managed
to get away.

It was not really a conscious plan that Marlboro made
to hoist himself over the high wall under the flyover
and crouch in the darkness within. He did not even
think about it before he did it; but there was in his mind
a difficulty with returning home: for how could he tell
Ona about all these things, and how could he not tell
her? And would it not be better for her if he was not
there when they came looking? For if the police did not
know who he was, there were other people who did and
he was no longer very sure how different all the apparently separate players in this game actually were.

Such were the thoughts in his head when he clam-
bered over that wall, when he squatted down in the vast
black chamber it had created and nestled among the
squashed vegetables and broken audio cassettes that
had been left. But something deeper was at work, for as
the sun rose to find him still crouching there, as the
workers returned to build still higher against the strip of
blue overhead, he could not bring himself to move, and
could only watch it all happen, as if from a great distance. There was still time for him to escape, call out to
one of them to help him climb out, even make an
attempt to scale the wall himself: there was still a gap
through which he could climb, at least communicate

with the outside world. But Marlboro had a lot on his mind, and perhaps he felt that, before he could return to his life, he would have to Understand; perhaps he was even looking forward to the moment when the cavern was sealed and there would be quiet and he would have more space than he had ever had for his mind to expand in.

As the gap closed, the familiar sounds of Balogun Market became more and more remote and even the cars rushing overhead and shaking the walls did not make much noise. The brick-by-brick ascent of the wall was calming in a strange sort of way and it helped him to think. Once in a while he could not stop himself from uttering aloud (how it echoed in such a large space!), 'Dearest Ona. I hope you become a great movie star.'

The Safehouse
Michel Faber

I

I wake up, blinking hard against the sky, and the first thing I remember is that my wife cannot forgive me. Never, ever.

Then I remind myself I don't have a wife anymore.

Instead, I'm lying at the bottom of a stairwell, thirty concrete steps below street level in a city far from my home. My home is in the past, and I must live in the present.

I'm lying on a soft pile of rubbish bags, and I seem to have got myself covered in muck. It's all over my shabby green raincoat and the frayed sleeves of my jumper, and there's a bit on my trousers as well. I sniff it, trying to decide what it is, but I can't be sure.

How strange I didn't notice it when I was checking this place out last night. OK, it was already dark by then and I was desperate to find somewhere to doss down after being moved on twice already. But I remember crawling into the rubbish really carefully, prodding the bin bags with my hands and thinking this was the softest and driest bed I was likely to find. Maybe the muck seeped out later on, under pressure from my sleeping body.

I look around for something to wipe my clothes with. There's nothing, really. If I were a cat, I'd lick the crap off with my tongue, and still be a proud, even fussy creature. But I'm not a cat. I'm a human being.

So, I pull a crumpled-up advertising brochure out of the trash, wet it with dregs from a beer bottle, and start to scrub my jacket vigorously with the damp wad of paper.

Maybe it's the exercise, or maybe the rising sun, but pretty soon I feel I can probably get by without these dirty clothes – at least until tonight. And tonight is too far away to think about.

I stand up, leaving my raincoat and jumper lying in the garbage, where they look as if they belong anyway. I'm left with a big white T-shirt on, my wrinkled neck and skinny arms bare, which feels just right for the temperature. The T-shirt's got writing on the front, but I've forgotten what the writing says. In fact, I can't remember where I got this T-shirt, whether someone gave it to me or I stole it or even bought it, long long ago.

I climb the stone steps back up to the street, and start walking along the footpath in no particular direction, just trying to become part of the picture generally. The big picture. Sometimes in magazines you see a photograph of a street full of people, an aerial view. Everyone looks as though they belong, even the blurry ones.

I figure it must be quite early, because although there's lots of traffic on the road, there's hardly any pedestrians. Some of the shops haven't opened yet, unless it's a Sunday and they aren't supposed to. So there's my first task: working out what day it is. It's good to have something to get on with.

Pretty soon, though, I lose my concentration on this little mission. There's something wrong with the world today, something that puts me on edge.

It's to do with the pedestrians. As they pass by me on the footpath, they look at me with extreme suspicion – as if they're thinking of reporting me to the police, even though I've taken my dirty clothes off to avoid offending them. Maybe my being in short sleeves is the problem. Everyone except me seems to be wrapped up in lots of clothes, as though it's much colder than I think it is. I guess I've become a hard man.

I smile, trying to reassure everybody, everybody in the world.

Outside the railway station, I score half a sandwich from a litter bin. I can't taste much, but from the texture I can tell it's OK – not slimy or off. Rubbish removal is more regular outside the station than in some other places.

A policeman starts walking towards me, and I run away. In my haste I almost bump into a woman with a pram, and she hunches over her baby as if she's scared I'm going to fall on it and crush it to death. I get my balance back and apologize; she says 'No harm done,' but then she looks me over and doesn't seem so sure.

By ten o'clock, I've been stopped in the street three times already, by people who say they want to help me.

One is a middle-aged lady with a black woollen coat and a red scarf, another is an Asian man who comes running out of a newsagent's, and one is just a kid. But they aren't offering me food or a place to sleep. They want to hand me over to the police. Each of them seems to know me, even though I've never met them before. They call me by name, and say my wife must be worried about me.

I could try to tell them I don't have a wife anymore, but it's easier just to run away. The middle-aged lady is on high heels, and the Asian man can't leave his shop. The kid sprints after me for a few seconds, but he gives up when I leap across the road.

I can't figure out why all these people are taking such an interest in me. Until today, everyone would just look right through me as if I didn't exist. All this time I've been the Invisible Man, now suddenly I'm everybody's long-lost uncle.

I decide it has to be the T-shirt.

I stop in front of a shop window and try to read what the T-shirt says by squinting at my reflection in the glass. I'm not so good at reading backwards, plus there's a surprising amount of text, about fifteen sentences. But I can read enough to tell that my name is spelled out clearly, as well as the place I used to live, and even a telephone number to call. I look up at my face, my mouth is hanging open. I can't believe that when I left home I was stupid enough to wear a T-shirt with my ID printed on it in big black letters.

But then I must admit I wasn't in such a good state of mind when I left home – suicidal, in fact.

I'm much better now.

Now, I don't care if I live or die.

Things seem to have taken a dangerous turn today, though. All morning, I have to avoid people who act like they're about to grab me and take me to the police. They read my T-shirt, and then they get that look in their eye.

Pretty soon, the old feelings of being hunted from all sides start to come back. I'm walking with my arms wrapped around my chest, hunched over like a drug addict. The sun has gone away but I'm sweating. People are zipping up their parkas, glancing up at the sky mistrustfully, hurrying to shelter. But even under the threat of rain, some of them still slow down when they see me, and squint at the letters on my chest, trying to read them through the barrier of my arms.

By midday, I'm right back to the state I was in when I first went missing. I have pains in my guts, I feel dizzy, I can't catch my breath, there are shapes coming at me from everywhere. The sky loses its hold on the rain, starts tossing it down in panic. I'm soaked in seconds, and even though getting soaked means nothing to me, I know I'll get sick and helpless if I don't get out of the weather soon.

Another total stranger calls my name through the deluge, and I have to run again. It's obvious that my life on the streets is over.

So, giving up, I head for the Safehouse.

II

I've never been to the Safehouse before – well, never inside it anyway. I've walked past many times, and I know exactly where to find it. It's on the side of town where all the broken businesses and closed railway stations are, the rusty barbed-wire side of town, where everything waits forever to be turned into something new. The Safehouse is the only building there whose windows have light behind them.

Of course I've wondered what goes on inside, I won't deny that. But I've always passed it on the other side of the street, hurried myself on before I could dawdle, pulling myself away as if my own body were a dog on a lead.

Today, I don't resist. Wet and emaciated and with my name writ large on my chest, I cross the road to the big grey building.

The Safehouse looks like a cross between a warehouse and school, built in the old-fashioned style with acres of stone façade and scores of identical windows, all glowing orange and black. In the geometric centre of the building is a fancy entrance with a motto on its portal. GIB MIR DEINE ARME, it says, in a dull rainbow of wrought iron.

Before I make the final decision, I hang around in front of the building for a while, in case the rain eases off. I walk the entire breadth of the façade, hoping to catch a glimpse of what lies behind, but the gaps between the Safehouse and the adjacent buildings are too narrow. I stretch my neck, trying to see inside one of the windows – well, it feels as if I'm stretching my neck, anyway. I know necks don't really stretch and we're the same height no matter what we do. But that doesn't stop me contorting my chin like an idiot.

Eventually I work up the courage to knock at the door. There's no doorbell or doorknocker, and in competition with the rain my knuckles sound feeble against the dense wood. From the inside, the pok pok pok of my flesh and bone will probably be mistaken for water down the drain. However, I can't bring myself to knock again until I'm sure no one has heard me.

I shift my weight from foot to foot while I'm waiting, feeling warm sweat and rainwater suck at the toes inside my shoes. My T-shirt is so drenched that it's hanging down almost to my knees, and I can read a telephone number that people are supposed to ring if they've seen me. I close my eyes and count to ten. Above my head, I hear the squeak of metal against wood.

I look up at the darkening façade, and there, eerily framed in the window nearest to the top of the portal, is a very old woman in a nurse's uniform. She flinches at the rain and, mindful of her perfectly groomed hair and pastel cottons, stops short of leaning her head out. Instead she looks down at me from where she stands, half-hidden in shadow.

'What can we do for you?' she says, guardedly, raising her voice only slightly above the weather.

I realise I have no answer for her, no words. Instead, I unwrap my arms from my torso, awkwardly revealing the text on my T-shirt. The sodden smock of white fabric clings to my skin as I lean back, blinking against the rain. The old woman reads carefully, her eyes rolling to and fro in their sockets. When she's finished she reaches out a pale, bone-wristed hand and takes hold of the window latch; without speaking she shuts the dark glass firmly between us and disappears.

Moments later, the massive door creaks open, and I'm in.

Even before the door has shut behind me, the sound of the rain is swallowed up in the gloomy interior hush of old architecture. I step uncertainly across the threshold into silence.

The nurse leads me through a red velvety vestibule lit by a long row of ceiling lamps which seem to be giving out about fifteen watts apiece. There is threadbare carpet underfoot, and complicated wallpaper, cracked and curling at the skirtingboards and cornices. As I follow the faintly luminous nurse's uniform through the amber passageway, I glance sideways at the gilt-framed paintings on the walls: stern old men in grey attire, mummified behind a patina of discoloured varnish like university dons or Victorian industrialists.

On our way to wherever, we pass what appears to be an office; through its window I glimpse filing cabinets and an obese figure hunched over a paper-strewn desk. But the old woman does not pause; if my admission to the Safehouse involves any paperwork it seems I'm not required to fill in the forms myself.

Another door opens and I am ushered into a very different space: a large, high-ceilinged dining room so brightly lit by fluorescent tubes that I blink and almost miss my footing. Spacious as a gymnasium and cosy as an underground car park, the Safehouse mess hall welcomes me, whoever I may be. Its faded pink walls, synthetic furniture and scuffed wooden floor glow with reflected light. And, despite its dimensions, it is as warm as anyone could want, with gas heaters galore.

At one end, close to where I have entered, two fat old women in nurses' uniforms stand behind a canteen counter wreathed in a fog of brothy vapour. They ladle soup into ceramic bowls, scoop flaccid white bread out of damp plastic bags, fetch perfect toast out of antique black machines. One of them looks up at me and smiles for half a second before getting back to her work.

The rest of the hall is littered with a hundred mismatching chairs (junk-shop boxwood and stainless steel) and an assortment of tables, mostly Formica. It is also littered with human beings, a placid, murmuring population of men, women and teenage children – a hundred of them, maybe more. Even at the first glimpse, before I take in anything else, they radiate a powerful aura – an aura of consensual hopelessness. Other than this, they are as mismatched as the furniture, all sizes and shapes, from roly-poly to anorexic thin, from English rose to Jamaica black. Most are already seated, a few are wandering through the room clutching a steaming bowl, searching for somewhere good to sit. Each and every one of them is dressed in a white T-shirt just like mine.

Behind me, a door shuts; the old nurse has left me to fend for myself, as if it should be transparently obvious how things work here. And, in a way, it is. The fists I have clenched in anticipation of danger grow slack as I accept that my arrival has made no impression on the assembled multitude. I am one of them already.

Hesitantly, I step up to the canteen counter. A bearded man with wayward eyebrows and bright blue eyes is already standing there waiting, his elbow leaning on the edge. Though his body is more or less facing me, his gaze is fixed on the old women and the toast they're buttering for him. So, I take the opportunity to read what the text on his T-shirt says.

It says:

JEFFREY ANNESLEY

AGE 47

Jeffrey disappeared on 7 April 1994
from his work in Leeds. He was driving
his blue Mondeo, registration L562 WFU.
Jeffrey had been unwell for some time and it was

decided he would go to hospital to receive treatment.

He may be seeking work as a gas-fitter.

Jeffrey's family are extremely worried about him.

His wife says he is a gentle man who loves

his two daughters very much.

'We just want to know how you are,'

she says. 'Everything is sorted out now.'

Have you have seen Jeffrey?

If you have any information, please

contact the Missing Persons Helpline.

Jeffrey Annesley reaches out his big gnarly hands and takes hold of a plate of food. No soup, just a small mound of toast. He mumbles a thanks I cannot decipher, and walks away, back to a table he has already claimed.

'What would you like, pet?' says one of the old women behind the canteen counter. She sounds Glaswegian and has a face like an elderly transvestite.

'What is there?' I ask.

'Soup and toast,' she says.

'What sort of soup?'

'Pea and ham.' She glances at my chest, as if to check whether I'm vegetarian. 'But I can try to scoop it so as there's no ham in yours.'

'No, it's all right, thank you,' I assure her. 'Can I have it in a cup?'

She turns to the giant metal pot on the stove, her fat shoulders gyrating as she decants my soup. I notice that the seams of her uniform have been mended several times, with thread that is not quite matching.

'Here you are, pet.'

She hands me an orange-brown stoneware mug, filled with earthy-looking soup I cannot smell.

'Thank you,' I say.

I weave my way through the litter of chairs and tables. Here and there someone glances at me as I pass, but mostly I'm ignored. I take my seat near a young woman who is slumped with her feet up on a table, apparently asleep. On the lap of her mud-stained purple trousers, a plate of toast rises and falls almost imperceptibly. The forward tilt of her head gives her a double chin, even though she is scrawny and small.

I read her T-shirt. It says:

CATHY STOCKTON
AGE 17
Cathy left her home in Bristol in July 2002
to stay in London. She has run away before
but never for this long. At Christmas 2003,
a girl claiming to be a friend of Cathy's
rang Cathy's auntie in Dessborough, Northants,
asking if Cathy could come to visit. This visit
never happened. Cathy's mother wants her

to know that Cathy's stepfather is gone now and
that her room is back the way it was.
'I have never stopped loving you,' she says.
'Snoopy and Paddington are next to your
pillow, waiting for you to come home.'
Cathy suffers from epilepsy and may need medicine.
If you have seen her, please call
the Missing Persons Helpline.

Cathy snoozes on, a stray lock of her blonde hair fluttering in the updraught from her breath.

I lean back in my chair and sip at my mug of soup. I taste nothing much, but the porridgy liquid is satisfying in my stomach, filling a vacuum there. I wonder what I will have to do in order to be allowed to stay in the Safehouse, and who I can ask about this. As a conversationalist I have to admit I'm pretty rusty. Apart from asking passers-by for spare change, I haven't struck up a conversation with anyone for a very long time. How does it work? Do you make some comment about the weather? I glance up at the windows, which are opaque and high above the ground. There is a faint pearlescent glow coming through them, but I can't tell if it's still raining out there or shining fit to burst.

The old woman who escorted me here hasn't returned to tell me what I'm supposed to do next. Maybe she'll escort somebody else into the hall at some stage, and I can ask her then. But the canteen ladies are cleaning up, putting the food away. They seem to have reason to believe I'm the last new arrival for the afternoon.

I cradle my soup mug in both my hands, hiding my mouth behind it while I survey the dining hall some more. There is a susurrus of talk but remarkably little for such a large gathering of people. Most just sit, staring blindly ahead of them, mute and listless inside their black-and-white texts. I try to eavesdrop on the ones who are talking, but I barely catch a word: I'm too far away, they have no teeth or are from Newcastle, Cathy Stockton has started snoring.

After about twenty minutes, a grizzled bald man walks over to me and parks himself on the chair nearest mine. He extends a hand across the faux-marble patio table for me to shake. There is no need for introductions. He is Eric James Sween, a former builder whose business had been in financial difficulties before he disappeared from his home in Broxburn, West Lothian, in January 1994.

I wonder, as I shake his surprisingly weak hand, how long ago his wife said she would give anything just to know he was safe. Would she give as much today? The baby daughter she desperately wanted to show him may be experimenting with cigarettes by now.

'Don't worry,' he says, 'it's a doddle.'

'What is?' I ask him.

'What you have to do here.'

'What do you have to do?'

'A bit of manual labour. Not today: it's raining too hard. But most days. A cinch.'

The old women seem to have melted away from the canteen, leaving me alone in the dining hall with all these strangers.

'Who runs this place?' I ask Eric James Sween.

'Some sort of society,' he replies, as if sharing information unearthed after years of painstaking research.

'Religious?'

'Could be, could be.' He grins. One of his long teeth is brown as a pecan nut. I suspect that if I could read the lower lines of his T-shirt, obscured by the table, there would be a hint of bigger problems than the failure of a business.

Which reminds me:

'No one must know what's become of me.'

Eric James Sween squints, still smiling, vaguely puzzled. I struggle to make myself absolutely clear.

'The people who run this place… If they're going to try to… make contact, you know… with…' I leave it there, hoping he'll understand without me having to name names – although of course one of the names is printed on my breast in big black letters.

Eric James Sween chuckles emphysemally.

'Nobody's ever gonna see you again,' he assures me. 'That's why you're here. That's why they let you in. They can tell you're ready.'

He is staring at me, his eyes twinkling, his face immobile. I realize that our conversation is over and I wonder if there is something I can do to bring it to a formal conclusion.

'Thank you,' I say.

I sit in my dining room chair for the rest of the afternoon, getting up occasionally to stretch my legs, then returning again to the same chair. No one bothers me. It is bliss not to be moved on, bliss to be left unchallenged. This is all I have wanted every day of my life for as long as I care to remember.

Everyone else in the hall stays more or less where they are, too. They relax, as far as the hard furniture allows, digesting their lunch, biding their time until dinner. Some sleep, their arms hanging down, their fingers trailing the floor. Some use their arms to make little pillows for themselves against the headrest of their chairs, nestling their cheek in the crook of an elbow. Others have their knees drawn up tight against their chin, perched like outsized owls on a padded square of vinyl. A few carry on talking, but by now I have reason to wonder if they are really talking to the people they sit amongst. Their eyes stare into the middle distance, they chew their fingernails, they speak in low desultory voices. Rather than answering their neighbours or being answered, they speak simultaneously, or lapse simultaneously into silence.

Eric James Sween, perhaps the most restless soul of them all, ends up seated in the most crowded part of the room, drumming on his thighs and knees with his fingertips, humming the music that plays inside his head. He hums softly, as if fearful of disturbing anyone, and his fingers patter against his trouser legs without audible effect. A little earlier, he found a handkerchief on the floor and wandered around the room with it, asking various people if it was theirs. Everyone shook their heads or ignored him. For a while I was vaguely curious what he would do with the handkerchief if no one accepted it, but then I lost focus and forgot to watch him. My concentration isn't so good these days. The next time I noticed him, he was hunched on a chair, empty-handed, drumming away.

Occasionally someone gets up to go to the toilet. I know that's where they're going because at one point a hulking arthritic woman announces to herself that she had better have a pee, and I follow her. She walks laboriously, obliging me to take childish mincing steps so as not to overtake her. I notice that on the back of her T-shirt she has a lot of text too, much more than on the front. In fact, there is so much text, in such tiny writing, that her back is almost black with it. I try to read some as I walk behind her, but I can't manage it. The letters are too small, and the woman is contorting her muscles constantly in an effort to keep her ruined body from pitching over.

She leads me to two adjacent toilet doors on the opposite end of the dining hall from the canteen. Fastened to one door is a picture of a gentleman in a frock coat and top hat; the other has a lady in a long crinoline dress, with a bonnet and parasol. I enter the gentleman toilet. It is bigger than I thought it would be and luridly white, more like a room in an art gallery. Above the washbasins is a faded illustration painted directly onto the wall; it depicts a pair of hands washing each other against a green medicinal cross. REINLICHKEIT, it says underneath.

I select one of a long row of teardrop urinals to stand at. They look ancient and organic, as if they have been fashioned from a huge quantity of melted-down teeth. There are caramel stains on the enamel like streaks of tobacco. Yet the drain-holes are bubbly with disinfectant, showing that they are clean.

I stand for a while at the urinal, giving myself permission to let go of my little reservoir of waste, but nothing happens, so I leave. At least I know how to find it now.

*

Finally it is time for the evening meal. The two old nurses arrive and start cooking, in the kitchen behind the canteen. A watery miasma emanates from their labours, floating out into the hall, ascending to the ceiling. There is a general murmur of anticipation. I go to the toilet, successfully clear my bowels, and find myself disturbed almost to tears by the softness of the toilet paper. I wash my hands under the sign of the green cross. A dark coffee of grime swirls in the sink, dilutes and gurgles away.

When I return to the dining hall, a queue is forming at the canteen counter. I wonder whether the Safehouse is the sort of set-up where all the really decent food is snatched by the early birds and there's only scraps and clammy leftovers for the latecomers. I take my place in the queue, even though I'm not particularly hungry. It's an opportunity to stand close behind someone, trying to read what's written on their back.

I'm standing behind a young man with bad acne on his neck and head. He has very short hair, like felt, lovingly clipped to avoid any trauma to all the bulbous little eruptions dotting the flesh of his skull. I wonder if a hairdresser charges a great deal more for that: to exercise such care, such restraint, such understanding. What has brought this young man here, if he so recently had a hairdresser who was prepared to handle his head so gently?

On the back of the young man's T-shirt is an unbelievable amount of text, a dense mass of small print which I can't imagine to be anything more than a random weave of symbols, a stylish alphabet texture. Starting near the top of his left shoulder, I read as much as I can before my attention wanes:

n:12/5/82, M:pnd(s), F:ai,

pM1:30/5/82}gs(!vlegLnd), hf8B,

M2:31/5/82}gs(!vlegLsd), @n7, gH, ^MGM:ingm, ¬b,

c(T)@m, pMGM3:4/6/82(v[#]penisd++), >@m, ¬X+,

Hn>j, pF4:8/12/82,

and so on and on, thousands of letters and numbers right down to his waist. I peek over the young man's shoulder, at the back of the woman standing in front of him, and then, leaning sharply out from the queue, I glimpse the backs of half a dozen people further on. They're all the same in principle, but some of them have text that only goes as far down as the middle of their backs, while others have so much that their T-shirts have to be longer, more like smocks or dresses.

My own T-shirt is pretty roomy, come to think of it. Definitely XL. I wonder what's on it.

There is a man standing behind me, a tall man with thick glasses and hair like grey gorse. I smile at him, in case he's been reading the back of my T-shirt and knows more than me.

'Lamb tonight,' he says, his magnified bloodshot eyes begging me to leave him be.

I turn and face front again. When my turn comes to be served, I am given a plate of piping-hot lamb stew. The fat nurse has dished it up in such a way that there is a big doughnut-shaped ring of mashed potato all around the edge of the plate, with a puddle of stew enclosed inside it. As she hands it over she smiles wanly, as if admitting she just can't help being a bit creative with the presentation, but maybe I'm reading too much into it. Maybe she's learned that this is the best way to prevent people spilling stew off their plates on their way back to the tables.

I sit down somewhere and eat the stew and the potato. There's quite a lot of lamb in the gravy and there's a few carrots and beans floating about as well. I haven't had anything this wholesome since my… well, for a long time anyway.

When it's all over, I stare into space. I'd meant to keep an eye on the others, to ascertain how much food the last ones in the queue got. But I forgot. My memory is not what it was; thoughts and resolutions crumble away like biscuits in a back pocket. The important thing is that no one is moving me on. I could weep with gratitude. Except of course I don't weep anymore.

After another little while, I become aware that the windows of the Safehouse have turned black. Night has fallen on the outside world. I feel a cold thrill of anxiety, the instinctive dread that comes over you when you realize you've foolishly put off the essential business of finding a soft enclave of rubbish or an obscure stairwell until it's too late. I imagine the bony old nurse coming up to me and saying it's time for me to go home now, and that the Safehouse opens again at ten o'clock tomorrow. But deep down I know this isn't going to happen. I'm here to stay.

I sit for another couple of hours, staring at the people but not really seeing them. I also stare at my shoes, mesmerised by the metal eyelets of the laces, the scuffs and grazes on the uppers. I stare at the black windows, the reflection of the fluorescent light on the table nearest me, the damp canteen counter, empty now. I wonder if I should be shamed or even alarmed by my lack of boredom. I hadn't realised before today how completely I have made my peace with uselessness. Out in the world, I was hunted from sitting-place to sitting-place, never still for more than an hour, often rooted out after a few minutes. In warm shopping malls detectives would lose patience if I loitered too long without buying; on stone steps outside shops people would swing the door against my back and say 'Excuse me'. Even at nights, watchmen would shine torches into my face, and unexpected vehicles would cruise close to my huddled body.

With so much outside provocation to keep me moving, I never noticed that inside myself I have, in fact, lost any need for action or purpose. I am content.

I wish my wife could know this.

Eventually a bell rings and people start filing out of the dining hall. I look around for Eric James Sween in case he might be making his way over to me to explain what happens now, but he's already gone. So, I fall into step with the others and allow myself to be herded into a new corridor.

It's a shabby passage, not very long. On one wall hang naïve paintings of meadows and farm animals, slightly skew-whiff and with incongruous gilt frames. The opposite wall is blank except for a very large laminated board, screwed securely into the plaster well above eye level. It looks like those lists you see in war memorials of soldiers who died between certain dates, or the lists of old boys in ancient universities. At the top, it says:

KEY TO ABBREVIATIONS

There are columns and columns underneath, five square feet of them, starting with:

> **n** = born
> **M** = mother
> **F** = father

PGM = paternal grandmother
MGM = maternal grandmother

and so on. I dawdle to a standstill under the board, allowing the other people to pass me. I read further down the columns, straining to understand and to remember. The further I read, the more complicated it gets. **p** means punished, for example, but it only really makes sense when learned in combination with other symbols, like **!**, meaning an act of physical violence.

I glance ahead. The last few columns are full of fearsome strings of algebra which, if I could decode them, would apparently explain highly complicated things involving social workers and police. Even the most compact-looking formula, $\{F\notin>M/\text{-}](\delta n^*)$, unfurls to mean 'birthday present sent by father, withheld by mother and never mentioned'.

I pull my T-shirt over my head, exposing my naked torso to the draughty corridor. The soft white fabric flows like milk over my fists as I try to get it sorted out. It's not the front I want to see: I know my name and I don't want to be reminded who might be worried about me. I hold the back of the T-shirt aloft and check its left shoulder. **n:13/4/60**, it says. That's my date of birth, right enough.

After that, it's hard going. My text makes no sense because I don't know what I'm looking at, and the key is no help because I can't see what I'm looking for. I try to tackle it one symbol at a time, hoping that a moment will come when it suddenly all starts falling into place. At least I have the advantage of having had quite a simple childhood.

Unfortunately, just as I'm a couple of lines into my text and am searching for an explanation for **pM9**, the ninth time my mother punished me, I feel a tap on my naked shoulder and almost jump out of my skin.

I spin around, my T-shirt clutched to my breast like a bath towel. Confronting me in the hollow corridor is the old nurse who admitted me to the Safehouse. My heart beats against my ribs as she glowers straight into me, face into face. Her withered hand remains raised, as if she is about to administer a Catholic blessing, but she merely scratches the air between us with a hovering fingernail.

'You mustn't take your garment off here,' she warns me, *sotto voce*.

'I was just trying to see what it says on my back,' I explain.

'Yes, but you mustn't.' Her eyes, fringed all round with dull silver lashes, glow like sad heirloom brooches. I cannot disobey her.

As I pull my T-shirt over my head, she retreats one small step to avoid my flailing arms. Then, when I'm decent again, she touches me lightly on the elbow, and escorts me along the corridor, away from the KEY TO ABBREVIATIONS board.

'It's bedtime now,' she says.

I am led into the Safehouse's sleeping barracks. It's an even larger space than the dining hall – more like some massive, echoing warehouse whose ceilings must accommodate the comings and goings of forklifts and cranes. It is harshly lit and draughty and smells like a vast kennel, with a faint whiff of chlorinated urine. The ceiling is so high that rafts of fluorescent lights are dangled on long chains, down to where the highest ladder might be able to service them. Each raft contains four strips nestled side by side. Suspended so far above my head, luminous, airborne and still, they remind me of childhood visits to the Natural History Museum – fibreglass dolphins and sharks, dusty with time and grimy at the seams.

I tilt my head back, trying to see beyond these glowing mobiles to the ceiling above. I glimpse the silhouettes of wooden beams and steel pipes, a shadowy Cartesian plane supporting a transparent, or at least translucent, roof.

I feel a prod at my elbow.

'Time for that later,' the old nurse chides me gently, and I walk on.

The floor we tread is an old pool of concrete worn

smooth as bone, silent under my feet. The rubber crêpe soles of the old nurse go *vrunnik, vrunnik, vrunnik* as she walks beside me, leading me deeper in.

I keep my eyes downcast, reluctant to see what this great warehouse is, after all, for. I feel a glimmering constellation of eyes on me, I fancy I can hear the massed sighing of breath.

'This is your bed, up here,' I hear the nurse say, and I have to look where she is pointing.

All along the walls, stacked like pallets of produce, are metal bunk-beds, a surreal Meccano bolted straight into the brickwork. The beds go twelve-high, each compartment a little nest of white sheets and oatmeal-coloured blankets. A few of these beds are empty, but very few. Almost every rectangular nook contains a horizontal human being – man, woman or child, installed like *poste restante*. Some lie with their backs already turned, their rumpled heads half-buried under bedclothes. But most stare straight at me, blinking and passionless, from all heights and corners of the room.

The old nurse is pointing at a vacant bed, eleven beds off the ground, which I can only get to by climbing an iron ladder up the side of the bunk tower. I look round at her awkwardly, wondering if I can bring myself to tell her that I have a fear of high places.

She purses her thin dry lips in what could almost be a smile as she waves her fingers brusquely upwards.

'No one falls here,' she lets me know. 'This is the Safehouse.'

And she turns and walks away, *vrunnik vrunnik, vrunnik.*

I climb the ladder to my bed. On the way up, I am conscious of my progress being watched by a great many people, and not just from a distance, but at close and intimate range by the inhabitants of each of the ten beds I climb past. Half in shadow, half illuminated by shafts of harsh light, they haul themselves onto their elbows, or merely turn their heads around on the pillow, staring hollow-eyed into my face as I ascend. They stare without self-consciousness, without mercy, reading what they can of the text on my T-shirt, or appraising my body as I haul it upwards only inches from their noses. Yet they stare, too, without any spark of real interest. I am an event, a physical phenomenon, occurring on the rungs of the ladder that is bolted to their own bunk. To ignore me would require a greater fascination with something else, and there is nothing. So, they stare, mute and apathetic, their gaze eyeball-deep.

Man or woman, they have all kept their T-shirts on, like white cotton nightgowns. I glimpse names and ages, and a word or two of history, incomprehensible without the remainder. Their other clothes are bundled up under their pillow – trousers, skirts, socks, even shoes, all to raise the level of the thin cushion in its envelope of stiff white cotton.

I reach the eleventh bunk and crawl in. Under cover of the sheet and blanket, I take off all my clothes except the T-shirt, and arrange them under my pillow like the other people here. I notice that my feet are quite black with dirt, that the flesh of the insides of my knees is scarred with a rash from sleeping too many nights in damp jeans, that my genitals are as small as a child's.

The sheet is so old and often-mended that I'm afraid of tearing it as I try to make myself comfortable, but the blanket is thick and soft. I wrap it around me, tucked snug around my neck, and am just about to make a decision about whether I'll pull it right over my head when the barracks falls into darkness.

Relieved to be invisible at last, I venture my head a little way out of my bunk, looking up at the ceiling. It is glass, as I'd thought: huge tessellated panes of tinted glass through which moonlight smoulders, indistinct and poorly defined. The dangling rafts of extinguished fluorescent tubes loom at black intervals in the air, suspended between me and the people on the other side. I stare into the gloom, waiting for my vision to adjust. But as soon as it does, and I begin to see pale shoulders and the feeble candlepower of wakeful eyes, I turn away. I don't know what I expected to see or what I expected to feel, but these shadowy towers of scaffolding, these tiers of hidden bodies and glow-worm faces, fail to strike awe or pity into my heart. This indifference shames me, or I imagine it ought to, and I make a conscientious attempt to feel *something*. After some effort, I decide that I feel gratitude, or at least absence of anxiety, owing to us all being here for the night, assigned to our places. Often since going missing I've daydreamed of going to prison, but of course the gift of brute shelter is not easy to earn. Whatever crime you may commit, the world still wants you to keep playing the game. Even murderers are visited by their wives and children.

I lay my head back on the pillow, quite carefully, for fear of dislodging my shoes and sending them plummeting to the floor below. The nurse was right, though: I feel no fear of falling myself. The rectangle of steel and wire on which I lie feels as secure as the ground. I relax.

Above me, there sags another mattress held in a metal web, bulging down under the weight of a heavy body. I reach up and touch the mattress and the metal that holds it, very gently, just for something to do. I wouldn't, for the world, wish to attract the attention of the sleeper above.

I close my eyes, and as my brain begins to shut down I realize that for the first time in months I don't have to worry about being found.

*

In the morning, after a blissfully dreamless sleep, I wake to the sound of coughing. From various recesses in the honeycomb of bunks, gruesomely distinctive snorts, hacks and wheezes are flying out. In time, I will come to recognize each cough and associate it with a name and a history. On that first morning, I know nothing.

I lean over the side of my bed and look down. On the floor far below, lit up brilliantly by the sunlight shining down through the transparent ceiling, is a silvery pool of urine. The metal towers of sleeping berths are mirrored in it; I scan our reflections trying to find myself, but can't tell the difference between all the tiny dishevelled faces. I raise one hand, to wave into the glowing pool, to clinch which one is me. Several hands – no, half a dozen – wave back at me.

I am no longer missing.

An Anxious Man
James Lasdun

Joseph Nagel slumped forward, head in hands.

'My God,' he groaned.

Elise snapped off the car radio.

'Calm down, Joseph.'

'That's four straight days since we got here.'

'Joseph, please.'

'What do you think we're down now? Sixty? Eighty thousand?'

'It'll come back.'

'We should have sold everything after the first twenty. That would have been an acceptable loss. Given that we were too stupid to sell when we were actually ahead—'

Joseph felt the petulant note in his voice, told himself to shut up, and plunged on:

'I did say we should get out, didn't I? Frankly, it was

irresponsible committing all that money—' *shut up, shut up* '—not to mention the unseemliness of buying in when you did—'

Oh God…

His wife spoke icily: 'I didn't hear you complain when we were ahead.'

'All right, but that's not the point. The point is—'

'What?'

Her face had tightened angrily on itself, all line and bone.

'The point is…' But he had lost his train of thought and sat blinking, walled in a thick grief that seemed for a moment unaccounted for by money or anything else he could put his finger on.

Elise got out of the car.

'Let's go for a swim, shall we, Darcy?'

She opened the rear door for their daughter and led her away.

Glumly, Joseph watched them walk hand in hand down through the scrub oaks and pines to the sandy edge of the kettle pond.

He gathered the two bags from their shopping expedition into his lap, but remained in the car, heavily immobile.

Money…For the first time in their lives they had some capital. It had come from the sale of an apartment Elise had inherited, and it had aroused volatile forces in their household. Though not a vast amount – under a quarter of a million dollars after estate taxes – it was large enough, if considered as a stake rather than a nest egg, to form the basis of a dream of real riches, and Joseph had found himself unexpectedly susceptible to this dream. The money he made as a dealer in antique prints and furniture was enough, combined with Elise's income from occasional web-design jobs, to keep them in modest comfort – two cars, an old brick house in Aurelia with lilac bushes and a grape arbour, the yearly trip up here to the Cape – but there wasn't much left over for Darcy's college fund, let alone their own retirement. In the past such matters hadn't troubled him greatly, but with the advent of Elise's inheritance he had felt suddenly awoken into new and urgent responsibilities. At their age they shouldn't be worrying about how to pay for medical coverage every year, should they? Or debating whether they could afford the dental and eye-care package too? And wasn't it about time they built a studio so that Elise could concentrate on her painting?

The more he considered these things, the more necessary, as opposed to merely desirable, they had seemed, until he began to think that to go on much longer without them would be to accept failure – a marginal existence that would doubtless grow more pinched as time went by, and end in squalor.

After probate had cleared and Elise had sold the apartment, they had gone to a man on Wall Street, a money manager who didn't as a rule handle accounts of less than a million dollars, but who, as a special favour to the mutual acquaintance who had recommended him, had agreed to consider allowing the Nagels to invest their capital in one of his funds.

Morton Dowell, the man's name was. Gazing out at the pond glittering through the pines, Joseph recalled him vividly: a tanned, smiling, sapphire-eyed man in a striped shirt with white collar and cuffs, and a pair of elasticized silver sleevelinks circling his arms.

A young assistant, balding and grave, had shown them into Dowell's cherry-panelled bower overlooking Governor's Island. There, sunk in dimpled leather armchairs, Joseph and Elise had listened to Dowell muse in an English-accented drawl on his 'extraordinary run of good luck' these past twenty years, inclining his head in modest disavowal when the assistant murmured that he could think of a better word for it than luck, while casually evoking image after image of the transformations he had wrought upon his clients' lives, and hinting casually at the special intimacies within the higher circles of finance that had enabled him to accomplish these transformations.

'I think it's just so much *fun* to help people attain the things they want from life,' he had said, 'be it a yacht or a house on St Bart's or a Steinway for their musical child…'

Joseph had listened, mesmerized, hardly daring to hope that this mighty personage would consent to sprinkle his magic upon their modest capital. He was almost overcome with gratitude when at the end of the meeting Dowell appeared to have decided they would make acceptable clients, sending his assistant to fetch his Sovereign Mutual Fund prospectus for them to take home.

'What a creep,' Elise had murmured as they waited for the elevator outside. 'I wouldn't leave him in a room with Darcy's piggy bank.'

Stunned, Joseph had opened his mouth to defend the man, but at once found himself hesitating. Perhaps she was right … He knew himself to be a poor judge of people. He, who could detect the most skilfully faked Mission desk or Federal-era sleigh bed merely by standing in its presence for a moment, was less sure of himself when it came to human beings. He tended to like them on principle, but his sense of what they were, essentially, was vague, unstable – qualities he suspected might be linked to some corresponding instability in himself. Whereas Elise, who had little interest in material things (and who had been altogether less unsettled by her inheritance than he had), took a keen if somewhat detached interest in other people, and was shrewd at assessing them.

Even as their elevator began descending from Dowell's office, Joseph had found his sense of the man beginning to falter. And by the time they got home it had reversed itself entirely. *Of course*, he had thought, picturing the man's tanned smile and sparkling arm-bands again; *what an obvious phony! A reptile!* He shuddered to think how easily he had been taken in.

'You know what? You should invest the money your-self,' he had told Elise.

'That had crossed my mind.'

'You should do it, Elise! It can't be that hard.' He was brimming with sudden enthusiasm for the idea.

'Perhaps I will give it a try.'

'You should! You have good instincts. That's all that matters. These money managers are just guessing like anyone else. You'd be as good as any of them.'

And this in fact had appeared to be the case. After biding her time for several weeks, Elise had made her move with an audacity that stunned him. It was right after the September 11 attacks, when the shell-shocked markets reopened. Over ten days, as the Dow reeled and staggered, she bought and bought and bought, icily resolute while Joseph flailed around her, wrenched between his fearful certainty that the entire capitalist system was about to collapse, his guilty terror of being punished by the gods for attempting to profit from disaster, and his rising excitement, as the tide turned and he could see, on the Schwab web page over his wife's shoulder, the figure in the Total Gain column swelling day after day in exuberant vindication of her instincts. An immense contentment had filled him. Thank God she had kept the money out of that fiend Dowell's clutches!

But then the tide had turned again. The number that had been growing so rapidly in the Total Gain column, putting out a third, a fourth, then a fifth figure, like a ship unfurling sails in the great wind of prosperity that had seemed set to blow once again across America, had slowed to a halt, lowered its sails one by one, and then, terrifyingly, begun to sink. And suddenly Elise's shrewdness, the innate financial acumen he had attributed to her, had begun to look like nothing more than beginner's luck, while in place of his contentment, a mass of anxieties began teeming inside him.

How exhausting it all was. How he hated it! It was as though, in investing the money, Elise had unwittingly attached him by invisible filaments to some vast, seething collective psyche that never rested. Having paid no attention to financial matters before, he now appeared to be enslaved by them. When the Dow or NASDAQ went down, he was dragged down with them, unable to enjoy a beautiful day, a good meal, or even his nightly game of chequers with his daughter. Almost worse, on the rare occasions when the indices went up, a weird stupor of happiness would seize him, no matter what awful things might be going on around him. And more than just his mood, the management of his entire sense of reality seemed to have been handed over to the markets. Glimpsing in the *Times* Business Section (pages that would formerly have gone straight into the recycling bin) an article on mutual funds bucking the downward trend, he had seen Morton Dowell's Sovereign Fund among the lucky few, and felt suddenly a fool for having allowed what at once seemed an act of astoundingly poor judgment to steer him away from that sterling, agile man…

God! All that and the nightmarish discovery that you could never get out once you were in anyway – couldn't sell when you were ahead because you might miss out on getting even further ahead, couldn't sell when you were down because the market might come surging back the next week, leaving you high and dry with your losses, though of course when it merely continued tanking you wanted to tear your hair out for not having had the humility to acknowledge your mistake, and salvage, sadder but wiser, what you could.

Whatever you did, it seemed you were bound to regret doing it, or not having done it sooner. It was as though some malicious higher power, having inspected the workings of the human mind, had calibrated a torment for it based on precisely the instincts of desire and caution that were supposed to enable it to survive. One could no more help oneself than the chickadee that nested in the lilacs outside their living room could stop attacking its own reflection in the window all day long every spring, however baffling and terrible every headlong slam against the glass must have felt.

Wearily, Joseph climbed out of the car.

In the kitchen, as he unpacked the grocery bags, he made a conscious effort to fight off his gloom. Four days into the vacation and he had yet to relax. It was absurd. The weather was perfect, the rented house peaceful, the freshwater pond it stood by clear as glass, the ocean beaches beyond it magnificent. And at three hundred dollars a day for the house alone he couldn't afford *not* to be enjoying himself.

His hand made contact with a soft, cold package inside one of the bags. Ah yes. Here was something one could contemplate with unequivocal relish: a pound and a half of fresh queen scallops for the grill tonight.

He had bought them at Taylor's, while Elise and Darcy shopped at the produce store next door.

Taylor's was one of the glories of the Cape, and as always, it had been packed that afternoon, vacationers crushed up against the zinc slope, anxiously eyeing the diminishing piles of snowy white bass fillets or glistening pink tuna steaks, guarding their place in line with one

foot while peering ahead to see what sandy gold treas-
ures lay in the day's salver of smoked seafood.

There had been an incident: two women had each
laid claim to the last pair of lobsters in the tank. The
woman who was first in line had been distracted,
searching for something in her purse, when the teenage
server came over. The other woman, tall and bronzed,
in an outfit of some tissuey material slung weblike
between thin chains of beaded gold, had silently held
up two fingers and pointed to the lobsters, which the
boy was already weighing for her when the first woman
realized what was happening. She protested that she
had been first in line, but the other woman simply
ignored her, handing the boy several bills with an
intense smile and telling him to keep the change, while
the boy himself stood in a kind of paralysis that seemed
as much to do with her immaculately constructed glam-
our training itself upon him at full beam as with the
awkwardness of the situation. 'We'll be gettin' more in
later,' he had muttered lamely to the first woman. 'Well,
gosh…' she had said breathily as the other woman, still
smiling, strode serenely out, the two live lobsters swing-
ing from her hand in their bag of crushed ice.

Joseph, who had observed it all, had felt vaguely that
he ought to stand up for the woman in front. But
nobody else had stirred and it didn't after all seem a
matter of great importance, so that in the end he had

done nothing, a fact of which he had felt fractionally ashamed as he left the store.

At any rate he had his scallops – huge, succulent ones, with their delicate-tasting pink corals still attached. Lucky he'd bought them before hearing the day's numbers, he thought, smiling a little. Otherwise he might have balked at the astronomical price Taylor's charged per pound. He stowed them away with a feeling of minor triumph, as if he had snatched them from the very jaws of the NASDAQ.

There was no sign of his wife and daughter when he made his way down to the pond. He stood on the small private jetty that came with the house, wondering if he were being punished for his comment about the timing of Elise's investments. Elise did have a punitive streak, and his comment had undoubtedly been offensive. Still, it was unlike her to vanish altogether without telling him.

A slight anxiety stirred in him. He fought it: he had noticed a growing tendency to worry recently, and he was aware that he needed to get a grip on it. They must have gone off to pick blackberries, he told himself, or maybe they had decided to walk over the dunes to the ocean. At any rate he would have his swim – across the pond and back – before he allowed himself to become concerned.

He stepped into the clear water, walked out up to his knees, then plunged on in, drawing himself forward with leisurely strokes. The top few inches of water were sun-warmed; below that it was abruptly cold. There were no other people around. Thumbnail-sized water-skimmers teemed on the surface ahead of him, thousands of them, jetting twitchily in every direction.

The 'pond' (he would have called it a lake) was a quarter mile wide. It took him twenty minutes to cross it, and by a determined effort of will he managed not to look back once to see whether Elise and Darcy had returned. At the far shore he climbed out to touch land, then turned around, half-believing that he would be rewarded for his self-control by the sight of figures on the jetty below their house.

There were none.

Easy now, he instructed himself as he waded in again. There was still the journey back before he was official-ly allowed to worry. But knowing that in twenty minutes you were going to legitimately succumb to anxiety was not very different from succumbing to it right now. He could feel in advance how, as he passed the halfway point on the pond, he would be seized by a mounting anger at Elise for not informing him of her plans, and how, as he swam on, the anger would change gradually to fear, which was worse because it indicated, did it not, that one's mind had reached some limit of reasonable hope and switched its bet from her and Darcy being perfectly, if irresponsibly, safe somewhere to their being caught up in some disaster.

How wearying, how humiliating it was to have so little faith in anything, to be so abjectly at the mercy of every tremor of fear in one's mind... Unballasted by any definite convictions of his own (convictions, he liked to joke, were for convicts), he appeared to have gone adrift in a realm of pure superstition. If I avoid listening to *Marketplace* for three days, the Dow will miraculously recover: It did not. If I close my eyes and hold my breath for seventeen strokes Elise and Darcy will be there on the jetty...

They were not.

He swam on, thrusting out violently from his shoulders, ropes of cooler water slipping around his ankles as he kicked back and down, as hard as he could, in an effort to annihilate the drone of his own thoughts.

The sun was low in the sky, banding every ripple he made with a creamy glaze. The light here! That was something else to relish. In the early morning it seemed to glow from inside the trees, spilling out from one leaf after another as the sun rose, a rich, gold-tinted green. In the afternoon it turned to this creamy silver. Then, it was the light itself one became aware of, rather than the things it lit. Right now, in fact, as Joseph looked across the pond, the glare of direct and water-reflected light was so bright he could no longer see the far shore. This seemed propitious, and he deliberately refrained from trying to squint through the dazzle, surrendering to it. He had caught this moment once or twice before on the pond, and it did have some mysterious, elevating splendour about it that took you out of yourself. Everything seemed purely an occurrence of light: the water streaming glassily as he raised each arm for its stroke, bubbles sliding over the curving ripples, the water-skimmers registering no longer as frantic insect hordes but careening saucers of light, the whole glittering mass of phenomena so absorbing it emptied your senses of anything but itself, and for a moment you had the impression you could not only see the light but taste it, smell it, feel it on your skin, and hear it ringing all around you like shaken bells.

Darcy was standing at the end of the jetty when he came through the glare. She was leaning over the water with a fishing net in her hand. Another girl was beside her, shorter and plumper, holding a yellow bucket. Behind them, a little further off along the beach, sat Elise, drawing in her sketchpad.

For a moment Joseph tried to resist the joyful relief that the sight offered (relief being just the obverse of the irrational anxiety of which he was trying to cure himself, and therefore equally undesirable), but it flooded into him. They were there! No harm had come to them! He swam on happily. How lithe and supple his daughter looked in her swimsuit, her legs growing long now, beautifully smooth, her brown hair already streaked gold from the sun.

A surge of love came into him, and with it a feeling of shame. How crazily out of perspective he had let things get, to have allowed money to loom larger in his mind than his own daughter! A few evenings ago she had been telling him in detail the plot of a film she had seen. He had pretended to be paying attention, but so preoccupied had he been with the day's losses that even his pretence had been a failure. With a pang he remembered the look of dismay on Darcy's face as she realized he wasn't listening to a word she was saying. How could he have done that? It was unforgivable!

The girls darted off as he approached the jetty, running down a path that led around the pond. Elise remained on her deck chair. She greeted him with a friendly look.

'Did you make it all the way across?' she asked.

'All the way. I see Darcy found a friend.'

'Yes. She's staying in the next house down. We're invited over for cocktails later on.'

'Cocktails. My!'

'I said we'd go. Darcy's so excited to have a play-mate.'

'Is she bored here?'

'No, but you know how it is…'

'I thought we might rent bikes tomorrow, and go whalewatching.'

'Interesting concept.'

'What? Oh!'

She was smiling at him. He laughed. Another of life's unequivocal pleasures: being reinstated in his wife's good graces. He rubbed himself dry. He felt refreshed, light on his feet.

An hour later he and Elise walked over to join their daughter at her new friend's house. A tall woman carrying a pitcher of purplish liquid greeted them on the deck.

'They call this a Cape Codder,' she said, holding her free hand out to Joseph. 'Hi, I'm Veronica.'

She was the woman he had seen earlier on in Taylor's.

She had changed out of the tissuey top into a sleeveless robe of flowing, peach-coloured linen, but Joseph had recognized her at once as the victor in the incident with the lobsters.

She poured the drinks and called into the house:

'Sugar…'

An older man came out onto the deck, sunburned, with a strong, haggard face and vigorous silvery tufts sprouting at his open shirt. 'Hal Kaplan,' he said, gripping Joseph's hand and baring a row of shiny white teeth in a broad smile.

Veronica poured drinks and the four adults sat at a steel table on the deck, while the girls played down by the pond. She spoke rapidly, her large eyes moving with an intent sociability between Elise and Joseph. Within minutes, she had sped the conversation past the conventional pleasantries to more intimate questions and disclosures, in which she took an unashamedly flagrant delight. She and Hal were each other's third spouse, she volunteered; they had met on a helicopter ride into the Grand Canyon. The girl, Karen, was Hal's daughter by his second wife, who had died in a speedboat crash. He and Veronica had been trying for a year to have a child of their own. There wasn't anything physically wrong with either of them, but because she was approaching forty and they didn't want to risk missing out, they had decided to sign up at an expensive clinic for in vitro fertilization, a process she described in droll detail, down to her husband's twenty-minute sojourns in the 'masturbatorium'. *Don't mind me*, her tone seemed to signal as she probed and confided, *I'm not someone you have to take seriously...* 'How about you guys...?' she asked. 'How did you meet?' As he answered, Joseph found himself thinking that if he hadn't seen her in Taylor's earlier on, he would have taken her for precisely the charmingly frivolous and sweet-natured person she seemed intent on appearing. And in fact he so disliked holding a negative view of people that he rapidly allowed his present impression of her to eclipse the earlier one.

Hal, her husband, had been an eye surgeon in Miami for twenty-five years. Now he was living, as he put it, on his 'wits'. Judging from the house they'd rented – bigger, sleeker and glassier than Elise and Joseph's – he was doing all right on them.

'Karen is in love with your daughter,' Veronica said to Elise, 'she is in *love* with her.'

Elise murmured that Darcy was thrilled too.

Swallows were diving over the pond, picking off skimmers. As the sun went down behind the trees the water turned a greenish black, with a scattering of fiery ripples. The girls came up, wrapped in towels, shivering a little. Elise looked at her watch.

'Why don't you stay and eat dinner with us?' Veronica asked.

Elise smiled: 'Oh no, we couldn't possibly…'

'It'd be no trouble, really.'

'Say yes, Mommy!' Darcy cried.

'We're just throwing some things on the grill. It seems a shame to break these two up…'

'Daddy could bring over our scallops…'

Elise turned to Joseph. Assuming her hesitancy to be nothing more than politeness, he made what he thought was the expected gesture of tentative acceptance.

'Well...'

And a few minutes later he was bringing the scallops over from their kitchen, along with a bottle of wine.

Hal had lit the grill. Joseph poured himself another Cape Codder and joined him.

'Lousy day on the markets,' he said, with a rueful chuckle.

The older man's long, rectangular face, full of leathery corrugations, hoisted itself into a grin.

'You play them?'

'We have a few little investments here and there.'

'Time to buy more, is what I say.'

'Oh? You think it'll go back up?'

'Like a rocket.'

'Really? Even the NASDAQ?'

'No question. The smart money's all over it. I'm buying like crazy right now.'

'You are?' Joseph's heart had given a little leap.

'You bet! Intel at twenty? Lucent under four dollars? These are bargain-basement prices by any estimation. Nortel at two fifty? Not buy Nortel at two dollars and fifty cents a share?' He gave another grin, the centres of his lips staying together while the edges flew apart, showing his teeth.

'That's extremely interesting,' Joseph said, enjoying

the unexpected feeling of well-being that had come into him. 'So you think a recovery's imminent?'

'Right around the corner, my friend. Right around the corner.'

It was like drinking a draught of some fiery, potent liquor!

Hal jostled at the coals in the barbecue with a two-pronged fork. He called over to Veronica:

'Bring 'em on, sweetheart!'

Veronica went into the kitchen and came out with the bag from Taylor's. Setting it on the table, she reached into the crushed ice and pulled out the two lobsters, one in each hand, and brought them over to the grill.

'Joseph, do me a favour and take the bands off, would you?'

She was holding the creatures out towards him.

Gingerly, he removed the yellow elastic bands from the flailing blue claws.

'Careful,' the woman said.

She caught his eye, giving him a sly, unexpected smile. Then she placed the living lobsters on the grill. Joseph had never seen this done before. The sight of them convulsing and hissing over the red-hot coals sent a reflexive shudder of horror through him, though a few minutes later he was happily eating his share.

*

At three that morning he woke up with a dry mouth and a full bladder. He got out of bed and walked unsteadily toward the bathroom. Through the open door to the living room he glimpsed the sofa bed where Darcy slept, and was momentarily stalled by the realization that it was empty. Then he remembered that she was sleeping over at her new friend's house.

A murky sensation, compounded of guilt and dim apprehension, stirred in him at the recollection of how this had come about.

He stumbled on into the bathroom, relieved himself, then stood in darkness, looking out at the pond. The moon had risen and the surface of the water, dimpled here and there by rising fish, shone brightly in its ring of black trees.

He had drunk too much, that was for sure, and overeaten. He recalled the weirdly euphoric mood that had mounted in him over the course of the evening: an unaccustomed exuberance. Partly it was Hal's amazingly confident predictions for the market. Several times Joseph had found himself steering the conversation back to the subject, raising various objections to the optimistic view, but purely for the joy of hearing this weather-beaten old oracle shrug them off. And partly, too, it was Veronica. With a few glances and touches she had deftly set a little subterranean current flowing between the two of them over dinner. He was a faithful husband, not even seriously tempted by actual bodily infidelity, but it gave him a tremendous lift to be flirted with by an attractive woman. Actually she wasn't, inherently, as attractive as he had first thought. Her chin was long and her nose looked as though it had been broken. But her evident conviction that she was desirable appeared to be more than enough to make her so. By the end of the evening he had been in an exhilarated state – drunk, aroused, glutted, his vanity flattered, his head spinning with the thought of the markets shooting back up 'like a rocket'.

As they had stood up to leave, Elise had called Darcy, only to be informed by the girls that Karen had invited her for a sleepover, and that she had accepted.

'Not tonight,' Elise had said, with more firmness than Joseph had thought altogether polite to their hosts.

The girls began appealing at once to the other adults. Veronica took up their case, assuring Elise that Darcy would be more than welcome.

'We *love* having kids stay over. Anyway, we're only a hundred yards away...'

Elise had looked to Joseph for support. Simultaneously Veronica had turned to him: 'It'll be so much fun for them, don't you think...?' She had laid her hand on his arm, and in the flush of his dilated spirits, he had announced imperiously that since they were on vacation, he saw no reason why Darcy should not sleep over.

Elise had said nothing; it wasn't her style to argue in public. But as soon as they were out of earshot, leaving their daughter behind with her new friend, she had turned on Joseph with a cold fury:

'First you force us to have dinner with those people, then you walk right over me with this sleepover. You are *un*believable.'

More than the fierceness of her tone, more than the aggrieved wish to remind her that it was she, not himself, who had accepted the original invitation to go over for cocktails, more than the bewilderment at her objecting so strongly to Darcy sleeping over with her new friend, it was her phrase 'those people' that had startled him. All this time, he realized, while he had been blithely enjoying himself, she had been assessing this couple, sitting in judgment on them, and quietly forming a verdict against them. On what grounds? he had wanted to know. But as he opened his mouth to demand an explanation he had felt once again the familiar sense of uncertainty about his own instincts.

And now, as he listened to the insomniac bullfrogs croaking down at the pond, the image of Veronica walking calmly out of Taylor's with the lobsters came back to him, and, with a guilty wonder at his wife's powers of intuition, he went uneasily back to bed.

*

The day was overcast when he awoke later. He was alone. As he opened the curtains he saw Elise striding up the steps from the pond. She burst in through the kitchen door.

'I am beyond angry.'

'What happened?'

'They've gone.'

'What do you mean?'

'They've gone. The car's not there.'

'With Darcy?'

'Yes, with Darcy.'

'No.'

'Yes.'

He felt a loosening sensation inside him.

'You checked inside the house?'

'The doors are locked. I yelled. There's no one there.'

Joseph threw on his bathrobe and ran outside, racing down the steps to the path. Rain had begun pattering onto the bushes. Reaching the other house, he blundered about the deck, beating on doors and windows and calling Darcy's name. The place was empty. The windows had screens on the inside, making it hard to see into the unlit interior, but what he couldn't see with his eyes his imagination supplied vividly: empty rooms, everything packed swiftly and surreptitiously in the dead of night, Darcy bundled into the car with the rest of them, then off out into the vastness of the country.

A feeling of terror swelled up inside him. He staggered back along the path and up the steps, legs shaking, heart pounding in his chest. Elise was on the phone.

'Are you calling the police?'

She frowned, shaking her head.

If she wasn't calling the police that must mean she didn't think things were as serious as he did. This calmed Joseph, though the calm had an artificial sheen to it that was familiar to him from the rare positive days on the Dow, as though some essential fact had been temporarily left out of the reckoning. Then he remembered again that Elise hadn't witnessed the scene in Taylor's, and it seemed to him suddenly that his wife had no idea what kind of people they were dealing with.

She hung up the phone and dialled another number. He realized she was calling nearby restaurants to see if their daughter's abductors had perhaps just gone out for breakfast. The idea seemed unbearably naïve to him. He stood there, helpless, immobilized, looking out through the thickening rain.

She hung up again:

'So much for that.'

'What are we going to do?'

'What do you propose, Joseph?'

'I think we should call the police. What kind of car did they have?'

'For god's sake! I don't even know their surname.'

'Call the police.'

'And say what? You call them.'

He picked up the receiver, but found himself reluctant to dial, as though to do so would be to confer more reality on the situation than he was ready to bear.

'Maybe just one of them went out and the other's still around here somewhere with the girls.'

'Doing what?'

'I don't know. Picking blackberries – or maybe they went to the ocean…'

'In this?'

'It wasn't raining earlier. Why don't I go check? You wait here…'

He ran out of the house again. The sandy path wound around the pond to a series of dunes – the trees giving way to wild roses, then sea grass with sharp edges that cut against his ankles. The sand crumbled under his feet as he climbed, half a step down for every step up. He was panting heavily as he reached the high point, his heart pounding in his ears. Wind whipped rain and salt spray into his face. He looked down at the shore. On sunny mornings the narrow margin between the dunes and the waves would already be covered with towels and fluttering beach umbrellas and little human figures in bright swimsuits – a touching image, it always seemed to Joseph: life blossoming fraily between two inhospitable elements. It was empty now, not a figure visible on the mile-long stretch of wet sand. Black waves came racing in with the wind, exploding onto the shore. Gulls flew screeching over the surf.

Was this it? Was this the catastrophe he had felt preparing itself inside him? His obscure, abiding sense of himself as a flawed and fallen human being seemed suddenly clarified: he was guilty and he was being punished. A feeling of dread gripped him. Childlike thoughts arose in his mind: propitiation, sacrifice... There was a clock, a valuable Crystal Regulator clock, that he had bought for a bargain in Asheville earlier that year. If their daughter was at the house by the time he got back, he would sacrifice the clock. He would destroy it: smash it to pieces in the back room of his store. Or no, better, he would return it to the dealer who had sold it to him, ask his forgiveness for taking advantage of him... And meanwhile, to show he wasn't only prepared to make a sacrifice in return for a guaranteed reward (the primitive religious state he had fallen into appeared to come complete with its own finer points of dogma), he vowed, right there and then, to change his entire life. Yes: he would devote himself to the poor and needy, give up drinking, overeating, flirting, obsessing about the markets, in fact he would tell Elise to sell off the shares and they would swallow the losses… The thought of this filled him with a sharp, almost painful elation: he seemed to glimpse in it the possibility of a new existence, one of immense and joyous calm. And even though he was aware in another part of himself that there was no prospect of his keeping a single one of these vows (that clock was earmarked to pay for this vacation), he turned back along the path full of faith and hope.

Veronica was at the house with the two girls when he arrived back. She was talking to Elise on the deck outside the kitchen. Seeing Joseph, she waved, laughing.

'We were playing in a tree house in the woods,' she called out. 'Hal drove into town to buy pastries.'

'Ah!'

'We always lock the door. Hal likes to keep a lot of cash around.'

'I see. I see.'

'We headed back as soon as we heard you guys yelling…'

She grinned at Joseph as he stepped onto the deck. She was wearing a white T-shirt and gold sneakers, her bare legs golden against the grey rain. A mischievous look appeared on her face:

'What were you thinking?'

He had had a moment of relief on seeing his daughter, but now he felt embarrassed.

'Nothing… We were just, you know, wondering where you were.'

She touched his arm, her eyes sparkling with hilarity.

'We freaked you out, huh?'

'No, no…'

He turned away, as though from an uncomfortably bright glare. Mumbling an excuse, he went on into the kitchen. Already his panic on the beach seemed absurd, shameful almost. What a state to get into! He turned on the radio. The *Marketplace* morning report was about to come on. Lifting a watermelon from the fridge, he set it on the counter and cut himself a thick slice. He ate it nervously while he listened.

The Ebony Hand
Rose Tremain

In those days, there was a madhouse in our village.

Its name was Waterford Asylum, but we knew it as 'the Bin'.

It appeared to have no policy of selection or rejection. If you felt your own individual craziness coming on, you could present yourself at the door of the Bin and this door would open for you and the kindly staff would take you in, and you would be sheltered from the cruel world. This was the 1950s. A lot of people were suffering from post-war sadness. In Norfolk, it seemed to be a sadness too complete to be assuaged by the arrival of rock'n'roll.

Soon after my sister, Aviva, died of influenza in 1951, my brother-in-law, Victor, turned up at the Bin with his shoes in a sack and a broken Doris Day record. He was one of many voluntary loonies, driven mad by grief. His suitability as a resident of Waterford Asylum was measured by his intermittent belief that this record, which had snapped in half, like burned, brittle caramel crust, could be mended.

Victor was given a small room with orange curtains and a view of some water-meadows where an old grey-white bull foraged for grass among kingcups and reeds. Victor said the bull and he were 'as one' in their abandonment and loneliness. He said Aviva had held his mind together by cradling his head between her breasts. He announced that the minds of every living being on the earth were held together by a single mortal and precarious thing.

I had a lot of sympathy for Victor, but I also thought him selfish – selfish and irresponsible. Because he abandoned his daughter, my niece, Nicolina, without a backward glance. It was as though he simply forgot about her – forgot that she existed. Nicolina walked home from school that day and did her homework, and ate a slice of bread and jam and waited for her father to turn up. There was no note on the table, no sign of anything out of the ordinary. Nicolina fed the chickens and did the ironing, and by that time it was dark. There was no telephone in that house. Nicolina was thirteen. She'd lost her mother less than a year back. Now, she sat in that Norfolk kitchen, watching the clock tick and listening to the owls outside in the black night. She told me that she sat there wishing she were five years old once more, eating salad cream sandwiches on her mother's lap. Then she found a torch and put on her coat, and walked the two miles to my house. 'Auntie Merc,' she said, 'my dad's gone missing.'

It was a cold November. We knelt by the gas fire, wondering what to do. We made ourselves sweet drinks out of melted Mars bars and milk. We wished we had a telephone or a car. We hoped that when morning came, normal life might be resumed. But some things are never resumed, not as they have been before, and my life was one of these things.

Nicolina was too young to live on her own in an empty house where her beautiful mother had once practised flamenco dancing and baked tuppenny silver charms into Christmas puddings, where her father had once come home from the war with gifts of nylon stockings and wind-up toys. So she stayed with me in the little brick bungalow where I'd lived alone for more years than I bothered to count. And I, who had no children of my own, or a husband, or anybody at all, tried to become a mother to Nicolina. I was forty-one years old. I had no idea how to be a mother, but I thought, well, in five or six years' time, Nicolina will find a husband and then I can hand her over to him. All I need to do is make sure this husband is a good one. I thought

I'd begin looking for him right away. And until then, I'd wash her hair on Friday evenings and save up for a radiogram. I'd tell her stories about Aviva and me when we were girls. I'd show her the picture of our Spanish grandfather who owned a bakery in Salamanca. I would try to love her.

She always called me Auntie Merc. Aviva and I had both been given Spanish names and mine was Mercedes. She – who had died at thirty-six – had been christened after life itself and I – who was unable to drive – had been christened after a car. Some of the people in our village still laughed out loud when they said my name.

Despite this, I was very fond of the village and never wanted to leave it. I couldn't imagine my life as a live-able thing anywhere outside it. I had a part-time job in a haberdasher's shop called Cunningham's. I enjoyed measuring out elastic and changing the glove display on an ebony hand which stood on the counter top. When Victor said what he said about our minds being held together by peculiar things, I thought to myself that the peculiar thing, in my personal case, was this wooden hand. It was well made and heavy and smooth. I polished it with Min cream once a week. I enjoyed the way it never aged or altered. And I began to think that this hand was like the kind of man I had to find for Nicolina: somebody who would not change or die.

*

On Saturdays, Nicolina and I would walk down to the Bin to visit Victor. We always took exactly the same route, through the village and out the other side on the road to Mincington, then made a short cut along a green lane than ran down to the water-meadows through orchards and fields.

There was one cottage on this lane, where a young man, Paul Swinton, lived with his mother, and it was often the case that when Nicolina and I came along, on our Saturday morning visits to Victor, Paul Swinton would be out working in the cabbage fields which bordered the lane. He would stop work and raise his cap to us and we would both say 'hello, Paul' and walk on. But one Saturday, after we'd walked on, I looked back and saw him staring at Nicolina. He was leaning on a hoe and gazing at her, at her pale hair tied in a ribbon and at her shoulders, narrow and thin, beneath her old green coat. And what I saw in this gaze was a look of pure longing and infatuation. And it was then that I thought that perhaps I had found him – before I'd officially begun my search – the good husband for Nicolina, whose feelings for her would stand the test of time.

I said nothing to my niece. On we went, down the hill to the meadows where the bull trudged round and round, then up the tarmac path to the gates of

Waterford Asylum, alias the Bin. We always took some gift to Victor, a jar of honey or a bag of apples. It was as if we couldn't let ourselves forget that Victor had come back from the war with his kitbag loaded up with presents cadged from the Americans. And I remember that on the day when I looked back to see Paul Swinton staring at Nicolina, we were carrying a basket of eggs.

When we gave the eggs to Victor, he took them all out of the basket, one by one, and arranged them on the windowsill in the sunshine, beside the orange curtains. 'They'll hatch out now,' he announced.

'Don't be a nerd, Victor,' I said. 'They're for eating, not rearing.'

He looked puzzled. His eyes darted back and forth from the eggs to Nicolina and me, sitting side by side on the bed, which was the only place to sit in Victor's tiny room. I looked at Nicolina, who would soon be fourteen and who was managing her life with fortitude. 'The eggs will go bad if you leave them in the sun, Dad,' she said quietly.

'No, no,' said Victor, 'your mother used to hatch eggs. In the airing cupboard. Turn them twice a day. She was full of wonders.'

Visits to Victor seldom went marvellously well. Sometimes, he seemed lost in a dream of an imaginary past. On the day of the eggs, he told us that he and Aviva had taken a cruise on the *Queen Mary* and that they had won the on-board curling championship and afterwards charvered in a lifeboat.

'What's "charvered"?' asked Nicolina.

'Dear-oh-dear,' said Victor, looking at his daughter with anguish. 'I see your mind is already turning to smut.'

'Shut up, Victor!' I said. 'If you can't control what you say, then don't talk.'

We sat in silence for a while. Nicolina took out a handkerchief from her pocket and wound it round and round her finger, like a bandage. Victor reached out suddenly and snatched the handkerchief from her hand. 'That belongs to your mother!' he bellowed.

'No ...' said Nicolina.

'I will not put up with people appropriating her things!'

'Calm down, Victor,' I said, 'or we'll have to leave.'

'Leave,' he said, folding the handkerchief very tenderly on his knee. 'Get the fuck out of my nest.'

When we got back to my house, Nicolina sat at the kitchen table, playing with two cardboard cut-out dolls she'd had since she was nine. These dolls had a selection of cut-out clothes that could be attached to their shoulders with paper tabs: polka-dot sundresses, white peignoirs, check dungarees, purple ball gowns. Nicolina referred to these dolls as her 'Ladies'. Now, taking the dungarees off the Ladies, leaving them in their pink underwear, she said: 'I wish I was a Lady. Then I wouldn't have to visit my father anymore.'

I didn't reply directly to this. But I crossed over to the table and picked up a ball gown and a paper tiara. 'These are lovely,' I said.

After her fourteenth birthday, I began to notice a change in Nicolina. She was gradually becoming beautiful.

When she came into Cunningham's, the old Cunningham sisters stared at her, like they sometimes stared at advertisements for millinery they couldn't afford. And now, every single Saturday, even when it rained, Paul Swinton waited for us, pretending to hoe his cabbages, and we would stand and have long conversations with him about the clouds or the harvest or the ugly new houses they were building along the Mincington road. As we chatted, I would watch his brown eyes wander over Nicolina's body and watch his hands, restless and fidgety, longing to touch her.

Nicolina and I never spoke about Paul Swinton. Though I knew he would one day become her kind and immovable husband, and believed I saw, in the way she stood so still and contained in front of him, that she knew this too, it seemed too soon to mention the subject. And I didn't want her to think I was counting the years until she left my bungalow, for this was not the case. My efforts to love Nicolina were succeeding fairly well. I began making her favourite fruit crumbles with tender care. When she was late home from school, I would start to feel a weight in my heart.

One Saturday in May, Nicolina refused, for the first time ever, to come with me to visit Victor. She told me she had revision to do for her exams. When I began to protest that her father would be upset not to see her, she put her arms round me and kissed my cheek, and I smelled the apple-sweetness of her newly washed hair. 'Auntie Merc,' she said, 'be a sport.'

I left her working at the kitchen table and went on my way to Waterford and when Paul Swinton saw that I was alone, he stood and stared at the lane behind me, hoping Nicolina would materialise like Venus from the waves of cow parsley.

I had no present for Victor that day and when I told this to Paul he took a knife out of his belt and cut a blue-green cabbage head and said: 'Take this and say it's from me and tell Victor that one day I'm going to marry Nicolina.'

A silence fell upon the field after these solemn words were spoken. I watched a white butterfly make a short, shivery flight from one cabbage to the next. I noticed that the sky was a clean and marvellous blue. Paul cradled the cabbage head in his hands. He stroked the veins of the outer leaves. 'Watching her grow and bloom,' he said, 'is the most fantastic thing that's ever happened to me.'

'I know,' I said.

'I've promised myself I won't invite her out or do anything to push myself forward until the time seems right.'

'I'm sure that's wise.'

'But I'm finding it difficult,' he added. 'How much longer do you think I have to wait?'

'I don't know,' I said. 'Perhaps until she's sweet sixteen?'

Paul nodded. I could imagine him counting the weeks and months, cold and heat, dark days and fair. 'I can wait,' he said, 'as long as, in the end, she's mine.'

With Nicolina's beauty came other things. She put her Ladies away in a box that was tied with string and never opened. She badgered me to buy the radiogram I still couldn't afford. I found one second-hand. Its casing was made of walnut and it was called 'The Chelsea'. And after that, Nicolina spent all her pocket money on Paul Anka records.

A boy called Gregory Dillon came round one teatime and Gregory and Nicolina danced in my front room to the song 'Diana'. They played the same record seventeen times. When they came out of the room, they looked soggy and wild, as though they'd been in a jungle.

'I think you'd better go home, Gregory,' I said. And he went out of the door without a murmur. It was as though dancing with Nicolina had taken away his powers of speech.

He came back a few days later, smelling of spice. His black hair was combed into a quiff, like Cliff Richard's, and his legs looked long and thin in black drainpipe trousers. He brought the record 'Singing the Blues' by Tommy Steele, but I told them to leave the door to the front room open while they danced to it. I sat in the kitchen, chopping rhubarb.

I've never felt more like singing the blues
Cos I never thought that I'd ever lose
Your love, dear...

Half my mind was on Nicolina and Gregory and the other half was on the changes occurring at Cunningham's, changes which might put my job in jeopardy. The two Miss Cunninghams were retiring and there was talk of the premises being sold to a fish-and-chip bar. That day, I'd gone to see Amy Cunningham and said to her: 'If the shop closes, please may I keep the ebony hand?'

'What ebony hand, Mercedes?'

'The hand for the glove display.'

'Oh, that. Well, I suppose so. Although, if it really is ebony, then it might be valuable. It might have to be sold.'

'In that case, I'll buy it.'

'What with? You spend every penny you earn on that girl.'

I'd never heard Nicolina referred to as 'that girl' before. I hated Amy Cunningham for saying this. I wanted to give her face a stinging swipe with a tea towel. 'I'll buy it,' I repeated, and walked away.

Yet when I got home and Nicolina and I were eating our tea in the kitchen, I raised my eyes and looked at her anew, as though I had been the one to call her 'that girl', and I saw that in among her beauty there was something else visible, something that I couldn't describe or give a name to, but I knew that it was alarming.

'Nicolina…' I began, but then I stopped because I hadn't planned what I was going to say and Nicolina looked at me defiantly over her glass of milk and said: 'What?'

I wanted, suddenly, to bring up the subject of Paul Swinton. I wanted to remind her that his hands were strong and brown, unlike Gregory's, which were limp and pale. I wanted to reassure her that I had been thinking about her future from the moment she'd come to live with me and that my vigilance on this subject had never faltered. But none of this could be said at that moment, so I started instead to talk about the clo-sure of Cunningham's and its replacement by a fish-and-chip bar.

'Does that mean,' asked Nicolina, 'that we'll have no money?'

I carried on eating, although I didn't feel hungry. I wanted to say: 'I suppose I knew that the young were heartless.'

It took quite a long time to complete the sale of Cunningham's, but because everybody in the village knew that it was going to close, fewer and fewer people came into the shop. It became a bit like working in a hospice for artefacts, where everything was dying. I began to feel a sentimental sorrow for the wools and bindings and cards of ric-rac. Every morning, I removed the glove from the ebony hand and dusted it. Sometimes, I held the naked hand in mine and I thought how strange it was that no man had ever want-ed to touch me and that I had never had a purpose in life until I became Nicolina's replacement mother. I stood at my counter, wondering what the future held. I tried to imagine applying for a job at the fish-and-chip bar, but I knew I wouldn't do this. I didn't like fish-and-chips. In fact, I didn't like food any more at all and I saw that the bones of my wrist were becoming as nar-row as cards of lace.

*

Not long after this, some months after Nicolina's fifteenth birthday, during a time when Elvis Presley's 'Love Me Tender' wafted out all evening from The Chelsea, I arrived at Cunningham's to find the ebony hand gone.

I searched through every drawer in the shop and unpacked every bag and box in the stockroom, and then I telephoned Amy Cunningham at home and said: 'Where is the hand you promised me?'

'I did not promise it, Mercedes,' said Amy Cunningham. 'And, as I thought, an antique shop in Stratton is prepared to give me a very good price for it. The hand is sold.'

I stood in the empty shop, unspeaking (as people did in the novels I sometimes took out of the Mincington library). I unspoke for a long time. A customer came in and found me like that, unspeaking and unmoving, and said to me: 'Where are your knitting patterns?'

The following day, Saturday, I couldn't get out of bed. I said to Nicolina: 'I'm sorry, but you'll have to go by yourself to see Victor.'

She stood at my bedside, wearing lipstick. She offered to bring me a cup of tea.

'No, thanks,' I said. 'I'm going to go back to sleep. Give your father my love.'

'What shall I take him?' she asked.

'I have no idea,' I said. 'You're on your own today.'

She looked at me strangely. Her lipsticked mouth opened a little and hung there open and I didn't like looking at it, so I turned my face to the wall.

'Auntie Merc,' said Nicolina, 'when you're better, can you teach me the flamenco?'

'No,' I said. 'I can't. Your mother was the dancer. Not me.'

The following Saturday, when we passed the cabbage field, there was no sign of Paul Swinton. I stopped on the lane, expecting Paul to appear, but everything was still and silent in the soft rain that was falling. Nicolina didn't stop, but walked on in the direction of Waterford, holding high a pink umbrella. She looked like a girl in a painting.

When we got to the Bin, the Senior Nursing Sister pounced on us and took us into her office, which had a nice view of a little lawn, where an elaborate sundial stood. I saw Nicolina staring at this sundial while the Senior Nursing Sister talked to us, and I understood that both of us had our minds on the same thing: the sudden, swift passing of time.

The Senior Nursing Sister informed us that Victor had fallen into a depression from which it was proving difficult to rescue him. He had broken his Doris Day record into shards and thrown away his shoes. He'd cut open his pillow and pulled out all the feathers and flung them, handful by handful, round his room. I privately thought that, at that moment, he must have looked like one of those ornamental snowmen, trapped inside a glass dome.

'Why?' I asked.

The Senior Nursing Sister sniffed as she said: 'Your brother-in-law had become accustomed to watching a white bull that was kept on the water-meadows. Our staff would sometimes be aware that, instead of addressing them, as reasonably requested, he was addressing the bull.'

Nicolina laughed.

'We knew about that old white bull,' I said. 'Victor imagined—'

'The bull has gone,' said the Senior Nursing Sister. 'We enquired of the farmer as to why it had been removed from the meadow and we were told that it had been put away.'

'What's "put away"?' said Nicolina.

'Gone,' said the Sister. 'Put out of its misery.'

I looked at Nicolina. We both knew that the Senior Nursing Sister was unable to talk about death, even the death of a bull. And I thought this could be one of the reasons why so many people came voluntarily to the Bin, because, there, the words which described the things that made you afraid were differently chosen.

'We've become alarmed that Victor might inflict harm on a fellow inmate,' said the Senior Nursing Sister, 'so we have had to move him.'

'Move him where?'

'To a secure room. We hope it may be a temporary necessity.'

Neither Nicolina nor I spoke. We stared at this woman, who was unobtrusively ugly, like me. We'd brought Victor a gift of twenty du Maurier cigarettes and I knew that we wouldn't be allowed to give these to him, in case he set fire to the soft walls which now surrounded him.

'What's going to become of him?' I said.

'He's receiving treatment,' said the Sister. 'We expect him to recover.'

We had no choice but to trudge home through the rain, and when we came in sight of the cabbage field, I thought perhaps Paul Swinton would be there and that the sadness we were feeling about Victor might lift a little with his breezy smile. But when we got to the green lane, Nicolina said: 'Let's go a different way. Let's go by the road and see the new houses.' And she went hurrying on, leaving me standing still as the sun came out and cast a vibrant light on her pink umbrella.

Things began to move quickly after that day, as though striving to catch up with time.

The Chelsea exploded one afternoon, and when I rushed into the front room to see what the bang was, there were Gregory and Nicolina doing the forbidden thing on the floor behind the sofa. Flames were beginning to lick the curtains, but Nicolina and Gregory stayed where they were, finishing what they had to finish, and when I turned on the fire extinguisher, Gregory's bottom was covered with foam, like fallen feathers.

That evening, when Gregory was gone and the fire was out, I told Nicolina she ought to be ashamed of herself. She picked her teeth and flicked what she found there onto the hearthrug. 'Are you listening to me?' I said.

'No,' said Nicolina. 'Why should I be ashamed of myself? Just because you never had a man? And anyway, I love Gregory. When I'm sixteen, we're going to get married.'

I felt very hot. I felt my blouse begin to stick to my back. 'What about Paul?' I said.

'Paul who?' asked Nicolina.

'Paul Swinton, of course. He told me he'd wait for you …'

'He knows that's pointless. He knows I'm marrying Gregory.'

'How does he know?'

'Because I told him.'

'Told him when?'

'That time when you were in bed. He started to say ridiculous things. I told him they were ridiculous. I told him I was soon going to be Mrs Gregory Dillon.'

I got up and went over to Nicolina. I tried to put my arms round her, but she pushed me away. 'I want better for you,' I said.

'Shut up, Auntie Merc!' she snapped. 'I'm going to get peeved with you if you crush me with stuff like that.'

In the nights, I lay in my narrow bed and wondered what to do. I thought of the life Nicolina would have with Gregory Dillon in some lonely city. I wished Aviva were alive to snap her castanets in Gregory's face and send him packing.

I contemplated trying to talk to Victor, but Victor had gone very silent since his time in the Secure Room. He sat by his window, smoking and staring at his feet in bedroom slippers. I took him a transistor radio and he held it close to his ear, like you might hold a watch, to hear its tick. He never asked about Nicolina and she never visited him anymore.

And on the green lane, there was never a sign of Paul Swinton. The cabbages grew and the sun shone on them and then, one day, they were cut and gone, and the leaves and roots left behind began to smell sour. It became irksome for me to walk that way.

On my last day at Cunningham's, before the removers came to take away what was left of the sewing silks and bindings, a woman came into the shop and sat down at my counter. It was Mrs Swinton, Paul's mother. She wore a choked expression, as though she found it difficult to swallow. She blinked very fast as she talked. She asked me to persuade Nicolina to change her mind and agree to marry Paul. I invited her to sit down on one of the last remaining leather chairs. 'Nicolina doesn't know her own mind,' I said. 'She's too young.'

'No,' said Mrs Swinton. 'Paul told me she was planning to marry somebody else. Some boy.'

'She's saying that in the heat of the moment. Because they dance and carry on. But it won't last. They're children.'

Mrs Swinton stared at me sternly, no doubt wondering how I could allow my niece to 'carry on' with anybody at the age she was. In her day, said this stare, nobody carried on in this village.

She opened her bag and took out a handkerchief and dabbed her eyes, which were brown, like Paul's. 'He's so unhappy,' she said. 'I don't know what to do. He's letting the land go to ruin.'

What came into me then was a sudden white-hot rage with Nicolina for breaking the heart of the man who loved her. 'Who do you think you are?' I wanted to scream at her. 'Just tell me who.'

'I'll talk to her,' I told Mrs Swinton. 'Tell Paul to try to be patient. It may all work out in the end.'

'I hope so,' said Mrs Swinton. 'The power of love to wound is a wretched business.'

After Mrs Swinton left, I stood alone in the shop, which had always been sweetly perfumed with mothballs, until it was almost dark. Then I walked home and found Nicolina in bed, weeping.

I tried to stroke her hair, but it was in a wild tangle, as though she'd attempted to pull it out. She screamed at me to leave her alone.

I went downstairs and, out of habit, melted a Mars bar with milk to make a hot drink. I imagined I was making it for Nicolina, but then I decided she wouldn't want a Mars bar drink right now, so I stood by the stove, drinking it myself. I longed for my dead sister to come alive again and walk in my door.

I switched on the wireless and a programme about the Camargue came on: a wild place full of white horses and bulrushes and empty skies, and I thought how lovely it would be to go there, just for a day, and smell the horse smell and the salt wind. I was so caught up in the programme that I didn't hear Nicolina come downstairs. But suddenly I looked up and saw a figure at the kitchen door and jumped right out of my cardigan, imagining it was Aviva's ghost.

Nicolina was wearing old check dungarees, a bit like the ones we used to dress her Ladies in. Her eyes were burning red.

'Gregory's gone,' she said.

'Sit down, Nicolina,' I said.

'I don't want to sit down.'

'Come on. Sit down and we'll talk about it.'

'I don't want to talk about it. He's gone. That's all. It's over. I'm only telling you because you need to know.'

She turned round then, as if to go back upstairs, but there she stopped and stared at me and said: 'There's something else. I'm pregnant. I expect you'll throw me out now. I expect you'll disown me.'

I spent the next weeks and months trying to reassure Nicolina. I told her I would repaint the little room at the back of my bungalow and make it into a nursery. I said a baby would be a novelty in my sheltered life. I said we would build a swing and hang it from the apple tree at the bottom of the garden. I said there was no chance of anybody being disowned. No chance.

Slowly, she came crawling out of her misery shell. She told me she was grateful for what I was doing. And, one Saturday morning in October, she agreed to come with me again to visit Victor.

We followed our old route over the fields. Nicolina made no protest about this. As we drew level with Paul Swinton's land, my heart began to beat unsteadily, wondering if he would be there, wondering if, when he saw Nicolina with her pregnant belly, he would try to do her harm. But there was no sign of him. The field was ploughed and empty soil. Yellow leaves from the hedgerows lay fallen there. It was as if Nicolina had known this is how it would be: just the blind earth, waiting for winter.

We went on, saying nothing, carrying our gifts for Victor, which consisted that day of some slices of cold pork and a bag of pear drops. We'd decided not to tell Victor about the baby. If you told Victor anything in advance of its being, he was unable to grasp it. It was as though the future were an enormous mathematical equation that had no meaning for him. Or perhaps time itself had no meaning for him any more. He hadn't seen Nicolina for months, but when we went into his room and she handed him the pork slices wrapped in greaseproof paper, all he said was: 'Aviva's hair was dark, but yours was always fair. I prefer the dark.'

She kissed his stubbled cheek and we sat down on the bed. Victor unwrapped the pork slices and began eating them straight away. Between mouthfuls he said: 'We've got a new resident. Younger than the rest of us. His name's Paul Swinton.'

I looked at Nicolina, but her face was turned away. She was holding onto a hank of her pale hair.

'I'm all in favour of new residents,' Victor continued, crunching on a sliver of crackling. 'They cheer me up.'

That night I couldn't sleep. Sorrow makes you weary, but never gives you rest.

I really didn't know how I was going to get through my future: the baby, the dirt and noise of it and having no money to buy toys. All I'd ever wanted was quietness. A life spent measuring elastic. I'd had forty-three years of a life I'd loved and now it was over.

The following day I took a bus to Stratton. A long time had passed since Amy Cunningham had sold the ebony hand to the antique shop there, so I told myself that it would be gone by now. But it wasn't gone. It was standing on a marble washstand, with a price tag of seventeen shillings tied round its thumb. And when I saw it and picked it up, a surge of pure joy made my head feel light.

There was only one problem. I didn't have seventeen shillings. I said to the shop owner: 'I'll give you what I have and pay the rest in instalments.'

The shop owner had a little chiselled beard and he stroked this tenderly as he regarded me, clutching the hand to my breast. 'How much have you got?' he asked.

I counted out eight shillings. He looked at this money and said: 'I'll take eight. It was sold to me as ebony, but it's not, of course. It's mahogany. It's just gone a bit dark with time.'

He offered to wrap the hand in brown paper, but I said this wasn't necessary. I carried it away, just as it was, held tightly in my arms. And when I got home, I brought out the Min cream and a duster and polished it till it shone, as it had always shone in the Cunningham's days. Then I placed the hand by my bed, very near my pillow, and lay down and looked at it.

I asked it to give me courage to go on.

Men of Ireland
William Trevor

The man came jauntily, the first of the foot passengers. Involuntarily he sniffed the air. My God! he said,
not saying it aloud. My God, you can smell it all right.
He hadn't been in Ireland for twenty-three years.

He went more cautiously when he reached the edge
of the dock, being the first, not knowing where to go.
'On there,' an official looking after things said, gestur-
ing over his shoulder with a raised thumb.

'OK,' the man said. 'OK.'

He went in this direction. The dock was different,
not as he remembered it, and he wondered where the
train came in. Not that he intended to take it, but it
would give him his bearings. He could have asked the
passengers who had come off the boat behind him but
he was shy about that. He went more slowly and they

began to pass him, some of them going in the same direction. Then he saw the train coming in. Dusty, it looked; beaten-up a bit, but as much of it as he could see was free from graffiti.

He was a shabbily dressed man, almost everything he wore having been abandoned by someone else. He had acquired the garments over a period, knowing he intended to make this journey – the trousers of what had been a suit, brown pin-striped, worn shiny in the seat and at the knees, a jacket that had been navy-blue and was nondescript now, the khaki shirt he wore an item once of military attire. His shoes were good, in one of his pockets was an Old Carthusian tie, although he had not himself attended Charterhouse. His name was Donal Prunty, once big, heavily made, he seemed much less so now, the features of a face that had been florid at that time pinched within the sag of flesh. His dark hair was roughly cut. He was fifty-two years old.

The cars were coming off the boat now, beginning to wind their way around the new concrete buildings before passing through one of them – or so it seemed from where he stood. The road they were making for was what he wanted and he walked in that direction. Going over, the livestock lorry he'd been given a lift in had brought him nearly to the boat itself. Twenty-three years, he thought again, you'd never believe it.

He'd been on the road for seven days, across the

breadth of England, through Wales. The clothes had
held up well; he'd kept himself shaven as best he could,
the blades saved up from what they allowed you in the
hostels. You could use a blade thirty or so times if you
wanted to, until it got jagged. You'd have to watch
whatever you'd acquired for the feet, most of all you
had to keep an eye on that department. His shoes were
the pair he'd taken off the drunk who'd been lying on
the street behind the Cavendish Hotel. Everything else
you could take was gone from him – wallet, watch,
studs and cufflinks, any loose change, a fountain pen if
there'd been one, car keys in case the car would be
around with things left in it. The tie had been taken off
but thrown back and he had acquired it after he'd
unlaced the shoes.

When he reached the road to Wexford the cars were
on it already. Every minute or so another one would go
past and the lorries were there, in more of a hurry. But
neither car nor lorry stopped for him and he walked for
a mile and then the greater part of another. Fewer
passed him then, more travelling in the other direction
to catch the same boat going back to Fishguard. He
caught up with a van parked in a lay-by, the driver eating crisps, a can of Pepsi Cola on the dashboard in
front of him, the window beside him wound down.

'Would you have a lift?' he asked him.

'Where're you heading?'

'Mullinavat.'

'I'm taking a rest.'

'I'm not in a hurry. God knows, I'm not.'

'I'd leave you to New Ross. Wait there till I'll have finished the grub.'

'D'you know beyond Mullinavat, over the Galloping Pass? A village by the name of Gleban?'

'I never heard of that.'

'There's a big white church out the road, nothing only petrol and a half-and-half in Gleban. A priests' seminary a half mile the other way.'

'I don't know that place at all.'

'I used be there one time. I don't know would it be bigger now.'

'It would surely. Isn't everywhere these times? Get in and we'll make it to Ross.'

Prunty considered if he'd ask the van driver for money. He could leave it until they were getting near Ross in case the van would be pulled up as soon as money was mentioned and he'd be told to get out. Or maybe it'd be better if he'd leave it until the van was drawn up at the turn to Mullinavat, where there'd be the parting of the ways. He remembered Ross, he remembered where the Mullinavat road was. What harm could it do, when he was as far as he could be taken, that he'd ask for the price of a slice of bread, the way any traveller would?

Prunty thought about that while the van driver told him his mother was in care in Tagoat. He went to Tagoat on a Sunday, he said, and Prunty knew what the day was then, not that it made a difference. In a city you'd always know that one day of the week when it came round, but travelling you wouldn't be bothered cluttering yourself with that type of thing.

'She's with a woman who's on the level with her,' the van driver said. 'Not a home, nothing like that. I wouldn't touch a home.'

Prunty agreed that he was right. She'd been where she was a twelve-month, the van driver said, undisturbed in a room, every meal cooked while she'd wait for it. He wagged his head in wonder at these conditions. 'The Queen of Sheba,' he said.

Prunty's own mother was dead. She'd died eighteen months before he'd gone into exile, a day he hated remembering. Word came in at Cahill's, nineteen seventy-nine, a wet winter day, February he thought it was.

'You've only the one mother,' he said. 'I'm over for the same.' Prunty made the connection in the hope that such shared ground would assist in the matter of touching the van driver for a few coins.

'In England, are you?' the van driver enquired.

'Oh, I am. A long time there.'

'I was never there yet.'

'I'm after coming off the ferry.'

'You're travelling light.'

'I have other stuff at Gleban.'

'Is your mother in a home there?'

'I wouldn't touch one, like yourself. She's eighty-three years of age, and still abiding in the same house eight children was born in. Not a speck of dust in it, not an egg fried you wouldn't offer up thanks for, two kinds of soda bread made every day.'

The van driver said he got the picture. They passed the turn to Adamstown, the evening still fine, which Prunty was glad about. He had two children, the van driver said, who'd be able to tell him if Kilkenny won. Going down to Tagoat on a Sunday was the way of it when old age would be in charge, he said; you made the sacrifice. He crossed himself when they passed a church, and Prunty said to himself he'd nearly forgotten that.

'You'd go through Wexford itself in the old days,' he said.

'You would all right.'

'The country's doing well.'

'The Europeans give us the roads. Ah, but sure she's doing well all the same.'

'Were you always in Ross?'

'Oh, I was.'

'I cleared off when I had to. A while back.'

'A lot went then.'

The van drew in when the conversation had been exhausted and there'd been silence for a few miles. They were in a quiet street, deserted on a Sunday evening. 'Well, there you go.'

'You couldn't see your way to a few bob?'

The van driver leaned across him to release the catch of the door. He pushed the door open.

'Maybe a fifty if you'd have it handy,' Prunty suggested, and the van driver said he never carried money with him in the van and Prunty knew it wasn't true. Reluctant to get out, he said: 'Any loose change at all.'

'I have to be getting on now. Take that left by the lamppost with the bin on it. D'you see it? Take it and keep going.'

Prunty got out. He stood back while the door was banged shut from the inside. They said it because the mention of money made them think of being robbed. Even a young fellow like that, strong as a horse. Hold on to what you'd have: they were all like that.

He watched the van driving away, the orange direction light flicking on and off, the turn made to the right. He set off in the direction he'd been given and no car passed him until he left the town behind. None stopped for him then, the evening sun dazzling him on the open road. That was the first time he had begged in Ireland, he said to himself, and the thought stayed with him for a few miles, until he lay down at the edge of a field. The night would be fine except for the bit of dew that might come later on. It wasn't difficult to tell.

The old man was asleep, head slumped into his chest, its white hair mussed, one arm hanging loose. The doorbell hadn't roused him, and Miss Brehany's decision was that she had no option but to wake him since she had knocked twice and still he hadn't heard. 'Father Meade,' she called softly, while the man who had come waited in the hall. She should have sent him away; she should have said come some time Father Meade would know to expect him; after his lunch when the day was warm he usually dropped off. 'Miss Brehany,' he said, sitting up.

She described the man who had come to the door. She said she had asked for a name but that her enquiry had been passed by as if it hadn't been heard. When she'd asked again she hadn't understood the response. She watched the priest pushing himself to his feet, the palms of his hands pressed hard on the surface of his desk.

'He's wearing a collar and tie,' she said.

'Would that be Johnny Healy?'

'It isn't, Father. It's a younger man than Johnny Healy.'

'Bring him in, Rose, bring him in. And bring me in a glass of water, would you?'

'I would of course.'

Father Meade didn't recognise the man who was brought to him, although he had known him once. He wasn't of the parish, he said to himself, unless he'd come into it in recent years. But his housekeeper was right about the collar and tie, an addition to a man's attire that in Father Meade's long experience of such matters placed a man. The rest of his clothing, Rose Brehany might have added, wasn't up to much.

'Would you remember me, Father? Would you remember Donal Prunty?'

Miss Brehany came in with the water and heard that asked and observed Father Meade's slow nod, after a pause. She was thanked for the glass of water.

'Are you Donal Prunty?' Father Meade asked.

'I served at the Mass for you, Father.'

'You did, Donal, you did.'

'It wasn't yourself who buried my mother.'

'Father Loughlin if it wasn't myself. You went away, Donal.'

'I did, all right. I was never back till now.'

He was begging. Father Meade knew, you always could; it was one of the senses that developed in a priest. Not that a lot came begging in a scattered parish, not like you'd get in the towns.

'Will we take a stroll in the garden, Donal?'

'Whatever would be right for you, Father. Whatever.'

Father Meade unlatched the French windows and went ahead of his visitor. 'I'm fond of the garden,' he said, not turning his head.

'I'm on the streets, Father.'

'In Dublin, is it?'

'I went over to England, Father.'

'I think I maybe heard.'

'What work was there here, all the same?'

'Oh, I know, I know. Nineteen… what would it have been?'

'Nineteen eighty-one I went across.'

'You had no luck there?'

'I never had luck, Father.'

The old man walked slowly, the arthritis he was afflicted with in the small bones of both his feet a nuisance today. The house in which he had lived since he'd left the presbytery was modest, but the garden was large, looked after by a man the parish paid for. House and garden were parish property, kept for purposes such as this, where old priests – more than one at the same time if that happened to be how things were – would have a home. Father Meade was fortunate in having it to himself, Miss Brehany coming every day.

'Isn't it grand, that creeper?' He gestured across a strip of recently cut grass at Virginia creeper turning red on a high stone wall with broken glass in the cement at the top. Prunty had got into trouble. The recollection was vague at first, before more of it came back: stealing from farms at harvest time or the potato planting, when everyone would be in the fields. Always the same, except the time he was caught with the cancer box. As soon as his mother was buried he went off, and was in trouble again before he left the district a year or so later.

'The Michaelmas daisy is a flower that's a favourite of mine.' Father Meade gestured again. 'The way it cheers up the autumn.'

'I know what you mean, all right, Father.'

They walked in silence for a while. Then Father Meade asked, 'Are you back home to stop, Donal?'

'I don't know am I. Is there much doing in Gleban?'

'Ah, there is, there is. Look at it now, compared with when you took off. Sure, it's a metropolis nearly.'

Father Meade laughed, then more seriously added: 'We've the John Deere agency, and the estate on the Mullinavat road and another beyond the church. We have the SuperValu and the Hardware Co-op and the bank sub-office two days in the week. We have Dolan's garage and Linehan's drapery and general goods, and changes made in Steacy's. You'd go to Mullinavat for a doctor in the old days, even if you'd get one there. We have a young fellow coming out to us on a Tuesday for the last year and longer.'

A couple of steps, contending with the slope of the garden, broke the path they were on. The chair Father Meade had earlier rested on, catching the morning sun, was still there, on a lawn more spacious than the strip of grass by the wall with the Virginia creeper.

'Still and all, it's a good thing to come back to a place when you were born in it. I remember your mother.'

'I'm wondering could you spare me something, Father.'

Father Meade turned and began the walk back to the house. He nodded an indication that he had heard and noted the request, the impression given to Prunty that he was considering it. But in the room where he had fallen asleep he said there was employment to be had in Gleban and its neighbourhood.

'When you'll go down past Steacy's bar go in to Kingston's yard and tell Mr Kingston I sent you. If Mr Kingston hasn't something himself he'll put you right for somewhere else.'

'What's Kingston's yard?'

'It's where they bottle the water from the springs up at the Pass.'

'It wasn't work I came for, Father.'

Prunty sat down. He took out a packet of cigarettes, and then stood up again to offer it to the priest. Father Meade was standing by the French windows. He came further into the room and stood behind his desk, not wanting to sit down himself because it might be taken as an encouragement by his visitor to prolong his stay. He waved the cigarettes away.

'I wouldn't want to say it,' Prunty said.

He was experiencing difficulty with his cigarette, failing to light it although he struck two matches, and Father Meade wondered if there was something the matter with his hands the way he couldn't keep them steady. But Prunty said the matches were damp. You spent a night sleeping out and you got damp all over even though it didn't rain on you.

'What is it you don't want to say, Mr Prunty?'

Prunty laughed. His teeth were discoloured, almost black.

'Why're you calling me Mr Prunty, Father?'

The priest managed a laugh too. Put it down to age, he said: he sometimes forgot a name and then it would come back.

'Donal it is,' Prunty said.

'Of course it is. What's it you want to say, Donal?'

A match flared, and at once there was a smell of tobacco smoke in a room where no one smoked anymore.

'Things happened the time I was a server, Father.'

'It was a little later on you went astray, Donal.'

'Have you a drink, Father? Would you offer me a drink?'

'We'll get Rose to bring us in a cup of tea.'

Prunty shook his head, a slight motion, hardly a movement at all.

'I don't keep strong drink,' Father Meade said. 'I don't take it myself.'

'You used give me a drink.'

'Ah no, no. What's it you want, Donal?'

'I'd estimate it was money, Father. If there's a man left anywhere would see me right it's the Father. I used say that. We'd be down under the arches and you could hear the rain falling on the river. We'd have the brazier going until they'd come and quench it. All Ireland'd be there, Toomey'd say. Men from all over and Nellie Bonzer too, and Colleen from Tuam. The methylated doing the rounds and your fingers would be shivering and you opening up the butts, and you'd hear the old stories then. Many's the time I'd tell them how you'd hold your hand up when you were above in the pulpit. 'Don't go till I'll give it to you in Irish,' you'd say, and you'd begin again and the women would sit there obedient, not understanding a word but it wouldn't matter because they'd have heard it already in the foreign tongue. Wasn't there many a priest called it the foreign tongue, Father?'

'I'm sorry you've fallen on hard times, Donal.'

'Eulala came over with a priest's infant inside her.'

'Donal—'

'Eulala has a leg taken off of her. She has the crutches the entire time, seventy-one years of age. It was long ago she left Ireland behind her.'

'Donal—'

'Don't mind me saying that about a priest.'

'It's a bad thing to say, Donal.'

'You used give me a drink. D'you remember that though? We'd sit down in the vestry when they'd all be gone. You'd look out the door to see was it all right and you'd close it and come over to me. "Isn't it your birthday?" you'd say and it wouldn't be at all. "Will we open the old bottle?" you'd say. The time it was holy wine, you sat down beside me and said it wasn't holy yet. "No harm," you said.'

Father Meade shook his head. He blinked, and frowned, and for a moment Miss Brehany seemed to be saying there was a man at the front door, her voice coming to him while he was still asleep. But he wasn't asleep, although he wanted to be.

'Many's the time there'd be talk about the priests,' Prunty said. '"The hidden Ireland" is Toomey's word for the way it was in the old days. All that, Father. "Close your eyes," you used say in the vestry. "Close your eyes, boy. Make your confession to me after."'

There was a silence in the room. Then Father Meade asked why he was being told lies, since he of all people would know they were lies.

'I think you should go away now,' he said.

'When I told my mother she said she'd have a whip taken to me.'

'You told your mother nothing. There was nothing to tell anyone.'

'Breda Flynn's who Eulala was, only a Romanian man called her that and she took it on. Limerick she came from. She was going with the Romanian. Toomey's a Carlow man.'

'What you're implying is sickening and terrible and disgraceful. I'm telling you to go now.'

Father Meade knew he said that, but hardly heard it because he was wondering if he was being confused with another priest: a brain addled by recourse to methylated spirits would naturally be blurred by now. But the priests of the parish, going back for longer than the span of Prunty's lifetime, had been well known to Father Meade. Not one of them could he consider, even for a moment, in the role Prunty was hinting at. Not a word of what was coming out of this demented imagination had ever been heard in the parish, no finger ever pointed in the direction of any priest. He'd have known, he'd have been told: of that Father Meade was certain, as sure of it as he was of his faith.

'I have no money for you, Prunty.'

'Long ago I'd see the young priests from the seminary. Maybe there'd be three of them walking together, out on the road to the Pass. They'd always be talking and I'd think to myself maybe I'd enter the seminary myself. But then again you'd be cooped up. Would I come back tomorrow morning after you'd have a chance to get hold of a few shillings?'

'I have no money for you,' Father Meade said again.

'There's talk no man would want to put about. You'd forget things, Father. Long ago things would happen and you'd forget them. Sure, no one's blaming you for that. Only one night I said to myself I'll go back to Gleban.'

'Do you know you're telling lies, Prunty? Are you aware of it? Evil's never forgotten, Prunty: of all people, a priest knows that. Little things fall away from an old man's mind but what you're trying to put into it would never have left it.'

'No harm's meant, Father.'

'Tell your tale in Steacy's bar, Prunty, and maybe you'll be believed.'

Father Meade stood up and took what coins there were from his trouser pockets and made a handful of them on the desk.

'Make your confession, Prunty. Do that at least.'

Prunty stared at the money, counting it with his eyes. Then he scooped it up.

'If we had a few notes to go with it,' he said, 'we'd have the sum done right.'

He spoke slowly, as if unhurried enunciation was easier for the elderly. It was all the talk, he said, the big money there'd be. No way you could miss the talk, no way it wouldn't affect you.

He knew he'd get more. Whatever was in the house he'd go away with, and he watched while a drawer was unlocked and opened, while money was taken from a cardboard box. None was left behind.

'Thanks, Father,' he said before he went.

Father Meade opened the French windows in the hope that the cigarette smoke would blow away. He'd been a smoker himself, a thirty-a-day man, but that was long ago.

'I'm off now, Father,' Miss Brehany said, coming in to say it, before she went home. She had cut cold meat for him, she said. She'd put the tea things out for him, beside the kettle.

'Thanks, Rose. Thanks.'

She said goodbye and he put the chain on the hall door. In the garden he pulled the chair he'd been sitting on earlier into the last of the sun, and felt it warm on his face. He didn't blame himself for being angry, for becoming upset because he'd been repelled by what was said to him. He didn't blame Donal Prunty because you couldn't blame a hopeless case. In a long life a priest had many visits, heard voices that ages ago he'd forgotten, failed to recognise faces that had been as familiar as his own. 'See can you reach him, Father,' Donal Prunty's mother had pleaded when her son was still a child, and he had tried to. But Prunty had lied to him then too, promising without meaning it that he'd reform himself. 'Ah sure, I needed a bit of money,' he said hardly a week later when he was caught with the cancer box broken open.

Was it because he clearly still needed it, Father Meade wondered, that he'd let him go away with every penny in the house? Was it because you couldn't but pity him? Or was there a desperation in the giving, as if it had been prompted by his own failure when he'd been asked, in greater desperation, to reach a boy who didn't know right from wrong?

While he rested in the sun, Father Meade was aware of a temptation to let his reflections settle for one of these conclusions. But he knew, even without further thought, that there was as little truth in them as there was in the crude pretences of his visitor: there'd been no generous intent in the giving of the money, no honourable guilt had inspired the gesture, no charitable motive. He had paid for silence.

Guiltless, he was guilty, his brave defiance as much of a subterfuge as any of his visitor's. He might have belittled the petty offence that had occurred, so slight it was when you put it beside the betrayal of a Church and the shaming of Ireland's priesthood. He might have managed to say something decent to a Gleban man who was down and out in case it would bring consolation to the man, in case it would calm his conscience if maybe one day his conscience would nag. Instead, he had been fearful, diminished by the sins that so deeply stained his cloth, distrustful of his people.

Father Meade remained in his garden until the shadows that had lengthened on his grass and his flowerbeds were no longer there. The air turned cold. But he sat a little longer before he went back to the house to seek redemption, and to pray for Donal Prunty.

Prunty walked through the town Gleban had become since he had lived in it. He didn't go to the church to make his confession, as he'd been advised. He didn't go into Steacy's bar, but passed both by, finding the way he had come in the early morning. He experienced no emotion, nor did it matter how the money had become his, only that it had. A single faint thought was that the town he left behind was again the place of his disgrace. He didn't care. He hadn't liked being in the town, he hadn't liked asking where the priest lived, nor going there. He hadn't liked walking in the garden or making his demand, or even knowing that he would receive what he had come for in spite of twice being told he wouldn't. He would drink a bit of the money away tonight and reach the ferry tomorrow. He wouldn't hurry after that. Whatever pace he went at, the streets where he belonged would still be there.

Biographical Notes

RANA DASGUPTA was born in Canterbury in 1971. Among his first memories are the shadowy pillars of the cathedral, in whose bookshop, on one early visit, his parents bought him a children's version of the *Canterbury Tales*.

Dasgupta grew up in Cambridge. He studied French literature at Balliol College, Oxford, and media studies at the University of Wisconsin. He then joined a marketing firm, which took him from London to Kuala Lumpur, and then to New York, where he ran the company's US operations. He now insists that business is a very good training for writers.

In 2001, Dasgupta moved to Delhi to write. He had made some initial sketches for a story cycle that would use folktale and myth as the language to explore the experiences and forces of globalisation. The book that came out of this, *Tokyo Cancelled*, was published in 2005.

It has so far been translated into eight languages, and one of the stories is currently being adapted for film by Australian screenwriter and director Robert Hutchinson. 'The Flyover' is taken from this book.

Dasgupta writes for several periodicals, including the *Guardian* and the *New Statesman*, and last year was commissioned to write 'The Horse', a short story for BBC Radio 4. He is currently working on his second novel.

MICHEL FABER was born in Holland in 1960. He moved with his family to Australia in 1967 and has lived in Scotland since 1992. His short story, 'Fish', won the Macallan/*Scotland on Sunday* Short Story Competition in 1996 and is included in his first collection of short stories, *Some Rain Must Fall and Other Stories* (1998), winner of the Saltire Society Scottish First Book of the Year Award.

His first novel, *Under the Skin* (2000), was shortlisted for the Whitbread First Novel Award and he has also won the Neil Gunn Prize and an Ian St James Award. Other fiction includes *The Hundred and Ninety-Nine Steps* (1999), a novella, and *The Courage Consort* (2002), the story of an a cappella singing group. His most recent novel, *The Crimson Petal and the White* (2002), creates a vast panorama of Victorian England and tells the story of Sugar, a 19-year-old prostitute.

A master of kaleidoscopic tones and styles, Faber is equally at home in the sprawling possibilities of the novel as he is in the concentrated realm of the short story – the form which allows him, he says, to get into 'as many different universes as possible.' His most recent short story collection is *The Fahrenheit Twins and other stories* (2005).

JAMES LASDUN is a British writer now living in the United States. He has published two collections of short stories, *The Silver Age* and *Three Evenings*; and three books of poetry, *A Jump Start*, *The Revenant*, and *Landscape With Chainsaw*, which was shortlisted for both the T. S. Eliot Prize and Forward Prize. He has written two novels, *The Horned Man* and *Seven Lies*. His awards include the Dylan Thomas Award for short fiction and a Guggenheim Fellowship in poetry.

Lasdun co-wrote the screenplay for *Sunday*, starring David Suchet and Lisa Harrow, which won both the Best Screenplay and the Grand Jury Prize for Best Feature at the Sundance Film Festival of 1997. His story 'The Siege' was adapted by Bernardo Bertolucci into the film *Besieged* and appeared in Lasdun's story collection of the same name in 1999.

ROSE TREMAIN has been publishing short stories since 1981. She has said of the short story: 'it's an exacting ' art. It demands a poetic coherence, a highly-tuned feeling for what's essential and what's superfluous.' She won the Dylan Thomas Short Story Award in 1984. She says she learned more about the form when teaching a course on 'The Great American Short Story' at Vanderbilt University in 1988 than in the rest of her working life.

Tremain has written nine novels including *Restoration*, winner of the *Sunday Express* Book of the Year Award and shortlisted for the Booker Prize. She was awarded the James Tait Black Memorial Prize and the Prix Femina Etranger (France) for *Sacred Country* and the Whitbread Novel of the Year Award for *Music & Silence*. Her most recent novel, *The Colour*, was shortlisted for the Orange Prize. Tremain's novels have been published in twenty-two countries and *Restoration* was filmed in 1995. Films of *Music & Silence* and *The Colour* are now in development.

Her acclaimed new collection, *The Darkness of Wallis Simpson*, was published by Chatto & Windus in 2005.

WILLIAM TREVOR was born in 1928 in Mitchelstown, County Cork, and spent his childhood in provincial Ireland. He attended a number of Irish schools and later Trinty College, Dublin, and is a member of the Irish Academy of Letters. He now lives in Devon.

His first novel, *A Standard of Behaviour*, was published

in 1958. His fiction, set mainly in Ireland and England, ranges from black comedies characterized by eccentrics and sexual deviants to stories exploring Irish history and politics, and he articulates the tensions between Irish Protestant landowners and Catholic tenants in what critics have termed the 'big house' novel. He is the author of several collections of short stories, and has adapted a number of his own stories for the stage, television and radio. These collections include *The Day We Got Drunk on Cake and Other Stories* (1967), *The Ballroom of Romance and Other Stories* (1972), *Angels at the Ritz and Other Stories* (1975) and *Beyond the Pale* (1981). His early novels include *The Old Boys* (1964), winner of the Hawthornden Prize, and *Mrs Eckdorf in O'Neill's Hotel* (1969). *The Children of Dynmouth* (1976) and *Fools of Fortune* (1983) both won the Whitbread Fiction Award, and *Felicia's Journey* (1994) won both the Whitbread Book of the Year and the *Sunday Express* Book of the Year Awards.

In 1999 William Trevor received the prestigious David Cohen British Literature Prize in recognition of a lifetime's literary achievement and in 2002 he was knighted for his services to literature. *The Hill Bachelors* (2000), a collection of short stories, won both the PEN/Macmillan Silver Pen Award for Short Stories and the *Irish Times* Irish Literature Prize for Fiction in 2001. *The Story of Lucy Gault* (2002) was shortlisted for the Man Booker Prize for Fiction. William Trevor's latest book, *A Bit On the Side* (2004), is a collection of short stories on adultery. He habitually describes himself as 'a short story writer who also writes novels.'